P9-EEB-508

Was this really the taciturn, disdainful Byrne Drummond, looking at her with unmistakable tenderness, with the same yearning she felt for him?

His right hand lay dark against the white sheet, mere inches from her thigh.

Burning up, she thought she might explode. She brushed the tips of her fingers against the edge of his hand, the merest feather-soft contact of skin against skin.

It was enough.

She felt fine tremors pass through him and then, with a soft groan, he leaned over her, touched his lips to hers.

Dear Reader,

In the Heart of the Outback... is a story about family, about feeling connected, about blood ties...and about belonging.

While writing this story, I found myself reexperiencing the miraculous gift of love that is part and parcel of family life—the love of a father for his daughter, of a sister for her brother, the love between husband and wife and the innocent, unquestioning love of a small child.

However, in this story, when tragedy strikes two families other emotions come to the surface—deep sorrow, naturally, but also hurt and pride, guilt and fear. I suffered along with my characters as they struggled with every setback, but the great thing about being an author is that I can make my characters stronger than I am.

I have to admit I fell for Byrne, an Outback cattleman and a strong and silent type, whose attractive, heroic qualities only emerge gradually as he lets down his taciturn facade.

And I admired the courage of Fiona, a hardheaded businesswoman who's succeeded in a man's world and yet is quite sure she will never be able to help Byrne face the difficult truth that binds their two families together.

It was a challenge to write this story, but such fun to help Byrne and Fiona overcome their obstacles. I hope you'll agree that this is a couple that has truly earned its very happy ending.

Warmest wishes from Down Under!

Barbara Hannay

BARBARA HANNAY

In the Heart of the Outback...

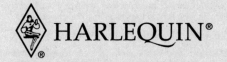

TORONTO • NEW YORK • LONDON
AMSTERDAM • PARIS • SYDNEY • HAMBURG
STOCKHOLM • ATHENS • TOKYO • MILAN • MADRID
PRAGUE • WARSAW • BUDAPEST • AUCKLAND

If you purchased this book without a cover you should be aware
that this book is stolen property. It was reported as "unsold and
destroyed" to the publisher, and neither the author nor the
publisher has received any payment for this "stripped book."

ISBN-13: 978-0-373-03946-3
ISBN-10:   0-373-03946-8

IN THE HEART OF THE OUTBACK...

First North American Publication 2007.

Copyright © 2007 by Barbara Hannay.

All rights reserved. Except for use in any review, the reproduction or
utilization of this work in whole or in part in any form by any electronic,
mechanical or other means, now known or hereafter invented, including
xerography, photocopying and recording, or in any information storage
or retrieval system, is forbidden without the written permission of the
publisher, Harlequin Enterprises Limited, 225 Duncan Mill Road,
Don Mills, Ontario, Canada M3B 3K9.

This is a work of fiction. Names, characters, places and incidents are
either the product of the author's imagination or are used fictitiously,
and any resemblance to actual persons, living or dead, business
establishments, events or locales is entirely coincidental.

This edition published by arrangement with Harlequin Books S.A.

® and TM are trademarks of the publisher. Trademarks indicated with
® are registered in the United States Patent and Trademark Office, the
Canadian Trade Marks Office and in other countries.

www.eHarlequin.com

Printed in U.S.A.

Barbara Hannay talks about her book:

"Just as I finished writing *In the Heart of the Outback*… relatives arrived from Canada, bringing with them a record of my family tree. Suddenly the world of my Scottish forebears became alive and real. I was fascinated by the colorful and interesting men and women who left Scotland for far-flung colonies in Canada, Australia and New Zealand, and I was reminded yet again of how wonderfully diverse families can be. And yet modern science and DNA have proved that all humans of every race are interlinked! After the weeks I'd spent with Byrne and Fiona and their families, this encounter with my own family seemed a fitting postscript."

Barbara Hannay was born in Sydney, educated in Brisbane and has spent most of her adult life living in tropical North Queensland, where she and her husband have raised four children. While she has enjoyed many happy times camping and canoeing in the bush, she also delights in an urban lifestyle—chamber music, contemporary dance, movies and dining out. An English teacher, she has always loved writing, and now, by having her stories published, she is living her most cherished fantasy. Visit her at www.barbarahannay.com

Don't miss Barbara's next book,
Needed: Her Mr Right
only from Harlequin Romance® this October
part of the **Secrets We Keep** trilogy

CHAPTER ONE

THE man standing a few feet from Fiona looked as haunted and desolate as she felt—too shocked to cry, too numb to feel pain.

He was wearing an oilskin coat, dark and shiny from the heavy rain outside, and he stood rock-still in the middle of the busy emergency ward, unaware of the staff ducking around him.

His skin was the suntanned brown of a man of the land, but shock had leached the tan from his cheeks. His eyes were dark and hollow, disbelieving. And although he was strong looking, tall and muscular, his shoulders were stooped, his chest caved in, as if the air had been sucked out of him.

He was clutching a teddy bear spotted with raindrops.

Fiona dropped her gaze and saw that the bottoms of his jeans and his riding boots were splattered with mud, and she wondered where he'd been when he was called to the hospital. She pictured him working in muddy stockyards, perhaps, dropping whatever task he was attending to—just as she had abandoned a board meeting in Sydney when the police had contacted her.

The horror in his face told her that his news had been terrible, too. She felt his shock, as deep and unexpected and dreadful as her own, and his stunned suffering seemed to double her awful anxiety about Jamie.

A nurse approached him. 'Mr Drummond?'

He didn't respond at first and the nurse tried again, more loudly. 'Mr Drummond.'

The nurse touched him on the elbow and he turned stiffly, his gaze fierce and threatening, his jaw jutting and rigid with tension. The nurse spoke to him in a quiet undertone, and Fiona watched the two of them set off down the ward. They looked incongruous—the tall, big-framed man with the tiny toy bear, following the short, dumpy nurse like an obedient child, like a robot programmed by remote control.

They disappeared, and Fiona was left with her own protracted nightmare.

She slid her jacket sleeve back from her wrist and glanced at her watch. It was four hours since she'd received the dreadful news of an accident on a remote road in Outback Queensland.

'I'm sorry to inform you that one of the victims is James Angus McLaren from Gundawarra,' the sergeant had told her. 'I believe you're his next of kin.'

Jamie, her brother, had been air-lifted to the Townsville Hospital, and his life now hung in the balance.

Shock had blunted her ability to think, but Rex Hartley, her company's senior partner, had been instantly sympathetic.

'Take the company jet,' he'd insisted, when he'd found her, white-faced, frantically trying to book a flight north. 'You need to get up there as quickly as you can.'

But, by the time she'd arrived at this emergency ward, Jamie had already been taken to an operating theatre and surgery had begun.

Since then, Fiona had paced these heavily disinfected corridors in an anxious daze, lost and shaken, scared sick and hollow with dread.

But she refused to think the worst. Jamie would pull through. Jamie always pulled through.

Her younger brother was like a cat with nine lives. His boyhood had been littered with countless accidents. He'd fallen from the garage roof, from his bicycle, from the frangipani tree. He'd broken his collarbone playing football, his ankle doing high-jumps, and he'd always bounced back, stronger and cheekier than ever. Jamie was invincible.

For heaven's sake, as an adult he'd flown 747's all over the world.

'Excuse me, are you Fiona McLaren?'

Fiona jumped and turned, saw a tired, young woman dressed in a white coat with a stethoscope looped around her neck, and she was swamped with sudden fear. Now she would hear how Jamie had fared. Her heart began to pound mercilessly.

The doctor introduced herself, but Fiona didn't catch her name. All she heard were the words that came next.

'I'm so sorry, Miss McLaren. We did everything we could. But your brother's injuries were too extensive.'

'No.'

Fiona whispered the word, but in her head she wailed it, and her loud, harrowing cry reverberated and echoed inside her. *No, no, no, no, no!*

Jamie couldn't be dead.

It wasn't possible. Her mind wouldn't, *couldn't*, accept that he was gone. She couldn't take it in.

She stared helplessly at the doctor's pale freckled face, waiting for the woman to clarify the mistake, to apologise for confusing her. This was a terrible dream. Surely she would wake to find these past four hours had been a long and cruel, drawn-out nightmare?

She heard the doctor say, 'There was a woman in the car. Tessa Drummond. Did you know her?'

'A woman?' Fiona frowned, trying to gather her wits. 'No, not at all.'

Jamie had only moved to Gundawarra two months ago, and he hadn't told her much about the people he'd met.

The doctor looked away and sighed. 'I'm afraid we couldn't save her either.'

Fiona's knees buckled at the thought that Jamie might have caused another death. As that dreadful possibility began to sink in, she felt an arm around her, supporting her.

'You need to sit down.' The doctor looked sympathetic. 'It's a terrible shock for you.'

Meekly Fiona nodded, and she was steered to a chair near a water cooler.

'I can offer you a glimmer of good news,' the doctor said gently as she handed her iced water in a paper cup. 'The little girl will be OK.'

Fiona stared up at her blankly. 'What little girl?'

The other woman frowned. Her head tilted to one

side as she regarded Fiona with narrowed, almost mys-
tified eyes. 'The little girl in the back seat. She was
wearing her seat belt, thank heavens. She's concussed,
but apart from that she hasn't a scratch.'

'I don't know anything about her,' Fiona protested.
'I don't know anything about any passengers. I—I
suppose they must have been friends of Jamie's.'

The doctor frowned again. 'There was no time to ask
questions. I'm sorry, I assumed… The child's blood is
AB—a perfect match with your brother's, and I—'

She stopped in mid-sentence as if she'd suddenly
realised she'd said too much. Clamping pale lips tightly
together, she shot a worried and puzzled glance down
the corridor.

Fiona remembered the man she'd seen standing there
a few minutes ago, looking shell-shocked and distraught
and clutching a teddy bear.

Was he the little girl's father?

She felt an unexpected need to explain. 'Jamie
doesn't—' She hesitated, but she couldn't bring herself
to say *didn't*. 'Jamie doesn't have any children.'

And then she remembered that Jamie would never
now have a chance to be a father, and she couldn't bear
it. Her body crumpled and she burst into tears.

Byrne Drummond leaned over the metal railing of the
hospital cot and placed a fluffy bear beside his daughter.

'Hey, Scamp.' He had to squeeze the words past the
painful log-jam in his throat. 'I brought you Dunkum.'

With great care he tucked the toy gently beneath the
sheet that covered her, but there was no flicker of response.

Byrne blinked to rid himself of the stinging in his eyes. His robust, bouncy little Scamp looked too vulnerable here in this sterile setting. Too neat and clean.

Where were the familiar smudges on her chubby cheeks? How had the nurses managed to get her hair brushed so tidily? It lay smooth and unruffled on the pillow, straight and brown, and neat as a pin. At home, at Coolaroo, Scamp had never stayed still long enough for Tessa to finish brushing her hair.

But look at her now.

So tiny and so still. So neat. So alone.

He touched work-roughened fingertips to her plump, pink cheek and felt a swift rush of relief. She was as warm as a baby bird, her skin super-soft. Gently, he pressed the backs of his fingers to her chest and felt her fragile rib bones and the valiant beating of her little heart. It was true, then. His daughter was warm and alive.

Despite what he'd been told by the doctors—that his daughter was merely concussed and that she was being kept in hospital for routine observations—he'd been too scared to believe. After seeing Tessa...

Oh, God.

Tessa...

A horrified groan broke from Byrne. He saw again the shocking image of his beautiful wife as she'd looked when they'd taken him to see her, and a chilling, cruel desolation sluiced through him. The worst kind of raw and jagged pain.

Unbearable horror.

Terrifying emptiness.

He was forced to clutch at the side of the cot. Through his tears, he looked with a kind of desperate hopelessness at the innocent face of his sleeping daughter. Poor, motherless Scamp.

If only he could save her from the devastating truth that awaited her when she woke.

It was mid-afternoon by the time Fiona finished with the police. She wasn't hungry—far from it—but there was a café in the hospital complex and, because she couldn't think what else to do, she went there and ordered coffee and a sandwich. But then she sat in a cloud of misery, leaving the coffee and the food untouched.

Think of something practical to do. Keep the memories at bay. Get busy.

Almost on cue, her mobile phone rang and she quickly retrieved it from the convenient pouch on the side of her handbag.

The caller was her PA, Samantha, checking in again to see how she was bearing up.

'Fair to middling.' Fiona forced brightness into her voice, and she filled Sam in on the details the police had provided. Jamie had given a lift to a mother and daughter from a neighbouring property. Their car had broken down and he'd offered to drive them home. But when he'd rounded a bend on a narrow Outback road he'd met a huge cattle train taking up most of the space.

It helped to talk about it. Fiona was Jamie's only sibling; their parents were both dead and she felt so horribly alone. Then she asked, 'How are things back at the office?'

'Mad as ever. But Rex asked me to tell you to take as long as you need to attend to your brother's affairs. The Lear jet is completely at your disposal.'

'That's good to know. Thanks. Anything else?'

'Well... Southern Developments have been on my back all morning. They want an assurance that you will manage their account.'

Fiona sighed. 'You'll need to explain to them that both Rex and I oversee the work we do for all our major clients, and this is a partnership. Rex acts for me. I act for him. Make that very clear to them.'

After Sam rang off, Fiona couldn't think what to do next.

Think, woman. Think or you'll sink.

Normally she prided herself on remaining level-headed and adaptable through any crisis. But this was different. This was Jamie. She sat, staring blankly at a poster without even noticing what it was advertising.

Her mind kept turning over everything the police had told her, like a scavenger searching through waste. What haunted her was the police sergeant's comment that an experienced driver should have been able to avoid that particular collision. Apparently, the driver of the cattle truck had sworn black and blue there'd been plenty of room for the two vehicles. He'd implied that Jamie must have been speeding. Or distracted.

Fiona couldn't imagine that Jamie would be reckless—not with passengers. So had he been distracted? If so, how? By the woman? Her child?

The possible answers to these questions gnawed at her, but she knew trying to guess the answer was pointless. Even if an inquest was held, no one could ever know exactly what had happened.

She thought again of the man she'd seen at the hospital, looking so shocked and devastated, clutching the teddy bear—thought of his little girl, the only survivor.

Byrne Drummond had lost his wife, the little girl her mother. The accident had wrecked that family.

And quite possibly Jamie was responsible.

Slumping forward, elbows on the table, Fiona pressed her fingers against her eyes to hold back tears. Losing Jamie was bad enough, but the thought of that family and the motherless child weighed on her. She remembered her father's death and her mother's incapacity to get on with life afterwards. It was from that point that Fiona had been forced to be strong. She'd mothered her little brother, had always felt responsible for Jamie.

And now, although she knew it wasn't quite rational, she couldn't help feeling a measure of liability and guilt for this accident. She heard again the implied blame in the policeman's voice, and the air in the café seemed to solidify around her, making breathing next to impossible.

Lurching to her feet, she paid for the coffee and sandwiches and hurried outside. But she felt no better as she rushed past the hospital's shops—past a newsagency, a bakery, a florist, a hairdresser.

A florist…

Fiona backtracked a few steps and studied the arrangements in the florist's window, peered through the shop and saw stuffed toys on a shelf on the back wall.

She made a swift decision. And immediately felt a little better.

* * *

'Riley's much brighter this afternoon. She's sitting up and getting bored. I'm sure she'd love a visitor.'

The sister in charge of the children's ward seemed only too happy to direct Fiona to Riley Drummond's room, which was decorated with a brightly coloured frieze of circus animals

The little girl was sitting in a cot, clutching a teddy bear in one arm, while she balanced a colouring book on her knees.

Using a fat bright crayon she was scribbling over a picture of a clown, with a cheerful disregard for rules about staying within the lines. She looked up as Fiona approached her nervously.

She had straight brown hair and round brown eyes set in a delightfully chubby face. For an instant, Fiona felt an uncanny sense of recognition, as if she'd seen that little face before somewhere.

But that was impossible. She was overwrought today; her imagination, strained to the max by her tumultuous emotions, was running haywire.

But she couldn't just stand there dithering. The child was watching her expectantly, waiting for her to speak.

'Hello, Riley,' Fiona began shakily.

The little girl eyed her solemnly. 'Hello.'

Only now, when it was far too late, Fiona regretted her limited experience of talking to small children. She'd always stayed well in the background whenever her friends were communicating with their offspring.

'Who are you?' the child asked.

'I'm Fiona. How are you feeling?'

Riley shrugged. 'A bit tired.' She gave a rather big yawn to prove it. 'Is my Daddy coming soon?'

'Your daddy?' She thought of the man in the emergency ward and felt a strange, inexplicable shiver. Caused by fear? Sympathy? Panic? 'I'm not sure where he is. He—he might be busy.'

Riley's lower lip pouted, and Fiona held her breath, wondering if the child would mention her mother. She felt another shiver. Perhaps this visit was a really bad idea. She was already out of her depth.

'Your daddy is probably on his way,' she amended.

'Can he take me home now?'

'Um… I'm afraid you'll have to ask the nurse about that.' Searching hurriedly for a safer topic, she asked, 'Where is your home?'

'Coolaroo.' Riley smiled as she looked up at Fiona. Her big, round brown eyes were touchingly trusting, and Fiona felt a swift, sharp pang of compassion for her.

Drawing up a chair, she sat beside her and opened a plastic shopping bag. 'I brought you this little fellow. I thought he might keep your teddy bear company.' She handed her a fluffy green-and-brown-striped toy.

It wasn't exactly pretty. In fact, it was verging on downright ugly, but for some reason Fiona had felt drawn to it when she'd seen it on the shelf at the back of the florist shop.

Riley, bless her, smiled at it. And then she giggled and poked its plush nose with a plump forefinger. 'It looks funny. What is it?'

'I think it's supposed to be a dinosaur.'

The little girl made a sound that was a mixture of laughter and growling. 'What's its name?'

'It hasn't got one yet. What's your teddy called?'

'Dunkum.'

'Duncan?'

'No. Dun-*kum*,' Riley insisted, with heavy emphasis on the '*m*'.

'Dunkum. That's a lovely name. Did you choose it?'

She nodded and smiled again, smugly.

'How clever of you.'

The child's eyes gleamed with delight and then mischief. Picking up the dinosaur, she squashed its face into the bear's. 'That means they're kissing and saying hello,' she explained, with an adorable, dimpling smile. And then, in a bossy voice, 'Say hello to Athengar, Dunkum.'

She looked expectantly at Fiona, who realised with dismay that she was expected to join in.

'Hello, Athengar.' Fiona managed this in a high-pitched, squeaky voice—a sound so alien, she was scarcely able to believe it had come out of her mouth.

But Riley sent her a quick smile of approval, and Fiona felt a flush of pleasure—the same flush of pleasure she normally felt when she pulled off a high-powered business deal. After all, this was her first attempt at playing with a child. And, for a moment, she'd stopped thinking about Jamie.

She'd actually remembered a toy from her own child-hood, an ugly camel she'd called Cazpar, that her father had brought home from a business trip as a surprise. Later, her mother had tried to throw it out, but she'd adored the thing and had clung to it so fiercely her mother had given in.

'Athengar's hungry,' Riley announced.

'Oh dear, what shall he eat?'

'You!' the little girl squealed, banging the toy against Fiona's arm and giggling wickedly.

Fiona's high-pitched squeal of mock terror was rewarded by a flash of genuine glee in Riley's eyes as if she was thrilled that this new grown-up companion was willing to join in her game.

They were both so busy giggling and squealing that at first they didn't notice the approach of heavy footsteps down the corridor.

But they couldn't ignore the very serious footsteps that marched into the room, accompanied by a fierce, wordless exclamation.

Fiona turned.

Byrne Drummond stood there, watching them.

From Fiona's seated position he looked imposing—taller and bigger than she'd remembered. Dark hair, grey eyes. Unsmiling. No—worse than unsmiling. He was angry and scowling—scowling at her.

Of course, he had every right to scowl at her. He'd just lost his wife and was hurting terribly. And her brother had been responsible for that pain.

Nevertheless, Byrne's anger was unsettling, and Fiona was grateful for the years she'd spent working with countless other unsettling, angry men. Now those experiences came to her aid, enabling her to rise with calm dignity, to meet Byrne Drummond's glare without flinching.

'What are you doing here?' he demanded through gritted teeth. The strain of his ordeal showed in the haggard vertical lines that bracketed his mouth.

'I wanted to pay Riley a visit,' Fiona said carefully, and then, less easily, 'I'm Fiona McLaren.'

'I know who you are. The nurse told me.'

He made no attempt to introduce himself.

'And you're Riley's father.' She said this calmly enough, but she felt as if she was walking through a minefield.

Byrne nodded, but his clear grey eyes glowered at her as if he wanted to add that it was none of her business.

Riley's perky little voice broke into the bubble of tension. 'Hello, Daddy.'

Byrne looked at his daughter and his face softened. He smiled at her, but it was such a bleak, struggling smile that Fiona felt her heart break for him.

She said, 'I only popped in for a brief visit.'

He showed no sign that he heard.

'Look what I got, Daddy.' Riley shook the dinosaur up at him. 'This is Athengar. Fee—fee—this lady gave him to me.'

Byrne slanted Fiona a black look, and then sneered at the fluffy toy as if it were a dirty, flea-infested rag. 'Looks like a cross between a lizard and a wombat.'

'He's a dinosaur,' Riley insisted, sounding offended. 'He's Athengar. He's Dunkum's new friend.'

Her father looked less pleased than ever.

Fiona watched the two of them, the warm, bubbly, brown-eyed child and the tall, handsome, stony-faced man with the attractive, lonesome cowboy aura. Until yesterday, there'd been another. Tessa Drummond. They'd been part of a threesome. A happy, warm little family.

Jamie's accident had changed all that.

She said, 'I'll go now.'

He nodded stiffly. 'I think that would be best.'

Fiona swallowed, bent down and picked up her jacket and the empty plastic bag that had held the toy. She managed a tight smile. 'Goodbye, Riley.'

''Bye.'

The little girl looked tired suddenly, and she cuddled the dinosaur close to her chest.

Fiona turned her attention to Byrne, looking him in the eye, hoping he might see her sincerity. 'Goodbye, Mr Drummond. Please accept my sympathy. I'm so sorry about your—' Just in time she remembered Riley. How much did this child know? 'I'm sorry about the accident.'

The fierce movement of his throat suggested that he couldn't respond even if he'd wanted to.

She drew a swift breath, in a bid for control, but her own loss of Jamie was too new, too raw. She couldn't be strong, couldn't hold back a sudden, fierce rush of grief. Her eyes filled with tears.

Byrne frowned fiercely, his eyes hard.

'Say goodbye to Athengar,' called Riley.

But Fiona couldn't. It had been a mistake to come. She'd achieved nothing.

She left quickly without looking back.

'Miss McLaren…'

Byrne found his voice just as Fiona disappeared. Through an opaque glass screen, he saw her silhouette freeze, and then she stepped backwards in an abrupt, jerky movement. And she was there again, framed in the doorway.

A snapshot from another world.

A redhead from the city in a slim beige skirt, a crisp white blouse, with tiny pearls at her ears and throat. Beige high-heel pumps and pale stockings emphasised her femininity. She held a silk-lined jacket, hooked by a finger and swinging from her shoulder.

On the surface, she looked cool, classy and collected, but she couldn't quite hide the vulnerability in her eyes.

But when her gaze met his, her nose lifted, like an animal scenting danger. Her green eyes narrowed and cooled, and she met his gaze levelly.

Only a raised eyebrow and very slightly parted lips hinted at the controlled curiosity with which she waited for him to speak.

Hell. For a fraught moment Byrne couldn't damn well remember why he'd called her back. He felt flickers of panic as his mind scrambled through a nightmare of tangled thoughts. *The accident. Tessa. Scamp. Oh, God. This redhead was the enemy. Related to the mongrel who —*

No. It was something practical. Ah, yes. He remembered...

'The property,' he said at last. 'What are you going to do with it?'

She frowned. 'Do you mean my brother's property? White Cliffs?'

'Yes.'

'I—I'm not sure. I haven't had time to think.'

She looked pale. Ill. He felt a moment's compassion, but then it was gone, buried beneath his pain.

'Why do you need to know?' she asked.

'White Cliffs shares my boundary, but it's been neglected. No fire breaks to speak of. A lot of the fences are in a bad way. I thought you ought to know it needs a bloody good clean up. And a decent manager.'

With a cool smile she said, 'Oh, don't worry, Mr Drummond. If I don't sell White Cliffs, I'll find a very good manager to look after it.'

He scowled at her. 'You'd better make sure it's someone who really understands the cattle business. Not like your brother.'

Fiona bristled visibly. Shoulders straightened, head high, she replied icily, 'So you were unhappy with my brother's—my *late* brother's—management of White Cliffs?'

'Out here we expect neighbours to pull their weight.'

'I don't need to be lectured on good management. You're worrying unnecessarily. I can assure you, one thing I'm very good at is hiring the right staff for specialised tasks.'

Byrne grunted. *Bully for you.*

He looked down at Scamp, who was lying down again, curled in her cot with her thumb in her mouth. The doctors had warned him she would be sleepy for a day or two.

'Don't you believe me, Mr Drummond?'

Across the room, Fiona McLaren's emerald eyes challenged him.

But Byrne was exhausted. In no mood for a battle. Drained. Almost too tired to hate her.

He dropped his gaze and shrugged. 'Time will tell.'

He was aware of her standing there, watching him for a long drawn out moment, as if she wanted to retaliate. But he didn't look her way again, and after a bit she turned and left, and this time she kept going. Byrne heard her high heels tapping and snapping all the way down the corridor to the front desk. And beyond.

He hoped he would never have to see her again.

CHAPTER TWO

FIONA's encounter with Byrne Drummond had proved one thing—she should leave attempts to express compassion and understanding to those with a talent for social work and empathy.

She, on the other hand, should concentrate on practical matters—Jamie's business affairs, for example.

Her brother had invested the money he'd made as a commercial airline pilot in the property at White Cliffs. Most of his business papers were out there, and it made sense to try to retrieve them before she went back to Sydney.

Realising there was a job to be done, she felt a little better. Byrne Drummond's bitter rejection still hurt, but she had business affairs to put in order and a Lear jet at her disposal. What was she waiting for?

Reaching for her cell phone, she called the airport. 'Hans, can you fly me to Gundawarra?'

Dusk found her still sitting at the desk in the front room of the White Cliffs homestead, trying to make sense of Jamie's very haphazard accounts.

The house was gloomy, and she got up to turn on a light, thought about making a cup of tea and hunting in the kitchen for something to eat. Her shoulders were stiff from hunching over files, and she stretched her arms high above her head, let them fall back to her sides and inadvertently tipped a manila folder from a shelf, knocking it to the floor.

Photographs spilled out on to the old fraying carpet.

Fiona bent quickly to retrieve them and saw that there were just three pictures. On top was a yellowing, black and white snapshot of a laughing little girl in an old-fashioned bathing costume.

The likeness to Riley Drummond was unmistakeable. Fiona felt an awful slam of panic. This little girl was the spitting image of Riley. They both had the same straight brown hair, chubby faces and big brown eyes. The set of their mouths and their serious, wise-little-owl expressions were identical.

And the thing that sent Fiona's heart reeling was the fact that she suddenly knew why Riley had seemed so familiar.

The child in the old black and white photo was her mother—Jamie's mother. She turned the photograph over and saw her mother's unmistakable handwriting on the back.

Me (Eileen) at Bondi Beach on my third birthday.

Before their mother had died she had divided up the family memorabilia very fairly into two albums for Fiona and Jamie—but Jamie had removed this photo from his album. Why?

Fearful now, Fiona looked at the next photo. It was of a group of young people, including Jamie, and he had his arm around the shoulders of a lovely young blonde. The photo had been taken at least five years ago, perhaps more. Fiona's eyes filled with tears as she looked down at her brother's face, laughing and carefree and alive.

A tidal wave of grief overwhelmed her and she melted to the floor, huddled and weeping helplessly.

Oh, Jamie, Jamie, Jamie...

Memories of him ran through her head like a non-stop movie reel... Jamie as a fun-loving, cheeky, little boy, as a handsome, restless teenager, as an adventurous young man with a trail of girlfriends beating a path to his door.

And tomorrow she had to take him back to Sydney. For a funeral. She couldn't, *couldn't*, bear it.

It was quite dark before she wiped her damp face and told herself that she was supposed to be dealing strictly with practical business matters. Photos aroused too many raw emotions.

But as she slipped the photos back into the folder, curiosity got the better of her. She turned the second photo over to read the names on the back. The name of the young woman with Jamie's arm about her shoulders was Tessa.

Tessa?

Shockwaves ricocheted through Fiona. Byrne Drummond's wife was called Tessa.

What was this about? A photo of their mother...of Tessa Drummond...

Surely it was a coincidence?

New, alarming possibilities leapt at her, making her ill. She was afraid to look at the last photograph. When she eventually turned it over, her heart rocked.

It was a picture of Riley Drummond. There could be no doubt. And she looked impossibly like the photo of their mother at the same age. This photo was in full colour, of course, and Riley was wearing modern shorts and a T-shirt and cuddling her teddy bear. But in every other way the resemblance was complete.

And, on the back, Jamie had written her name: *Riley Drummond*.

What did this mean?

There had to be a sensible explanation. The likeness was a strange, inexplicable coincidence. Jamie had been stunned when he'd seen his new neighbour's little girl and he'd retrieved their mother's photo for comparison.

And yet, that didn't explain why he'd also kept a photo of himself with a woman called Tessa.

Fiona almost gagged on the surge of dismay that filled her throat as she remembered something the doctor at the hospital had said this morning—something about a blood-group match between Riley and Jamie. The doctor had seemed startled to learn that Riley was not Jamie's daughter.

The child's blood is AB—a perfect match with your brother's...

Surely not.

Jamie couldn't have been Riley Drummond's father.

Fiona thought of Byrne Drummond's anger. Was there more behind his animosity than she'd realised? She remembered the awful anguish she'd witnessed in his handsome face in the emergency ward. In spite of the harshness of their more recent encounter, she doubted she would ever forget the poignancy of that first image, of him standing there, clutching the child's bear.

His pain had been so visible and it had tugged at her heart.

He was Tessa Drummond's husband and he was the little girl's father.

Not Jamie.

Never Jamie.

Shoving the wretched photos back into the folder, Fiona staggered to the nearest window, suddenly ill and needing air. The old timber-framed casement wouldn't budge at first, but eventually she got it open.

Beyond the homestead there was nothing but bush and warm, clammy tropical air. An incredibly loud and shrill chorus of cicadas hurt her ears. Mosquitoes buzzed. The moon, already riding high above the tops of the gum trees, lit up their trunks with ghostly silver, giving them a sinister, eerie beauty. From somewhere in the dark beyond the stand of trees, a cow bellowed mournfully.

Fiona wondered why Jamie had liked this place so much. She much preferred her slick downtown Sydney apartment with its aluminium and glass windows and fitted insect screens, with the constant hum of traffic and views of bright neon lights and skyscrapers.

Turning back into the house, she felt emotionally exhausted. And unexpectedly afraid. Not only had she lost her brother, but he'd left behind a distressing mystery.

Who else might know this? It seemed too great a burden to bear alone.

She wished she'd never seen those photos. They were

none of her business, and she didn't want to know what they meant.

Worrying about them would keep her awake all night, as would the even bigger question...

Had Byrne Drummond seen them?

CHAPTER THREE

HALFWAY up the brightly lit steps of the Gundawarra Social Club hall, Byrne, dressed in a black dinner suit, starched white evening shirt and elegant black bow tie, came to an abrupt stop, paralysed by second thoughts.

'Come on, mate. You can't back out now.'

His friends were adamant. After three years, it was high time he ventured back into society.

'You aren't Queen Victoria, Byrne. You can't stay in mourning for ever.'

There had been unanimous agreement that Gundawarra's Spring Ball was the perfect occasion for Byrne to 'come out'. It would be a masked ball, so everyone would be in disguise. Byrne could remain incognito for the first half of the evening, and by the time he had to unmask he'd have thawed out.

'You'll be your old self. A regular Prince Charming. We won't be able to get near you for women.'

The idea had sounded harmless enough as he and his mates had drunk sundowners on his homestead verandah. But now that he was actually here, listening to the strains of a dance band, the clink of glassware and bright ripples of laughter, Byrne wasn't so sure.

For the past three years, since his wife's death, he'd lived a reclusive life at Coolaroo with his daughter and the Jacksons, a quiet and kindly elderly couple. Ellen and Ted teamed as his housekeeper and general handyman and, on the rare occasions that he went out, they doubled as his babysitters. But the only social events he'd attended since the accident had been private affairs at friends' homes—small dinners or family barbecues.

Now this.

In a moment of weakness he'd been talked into attending the biggest event on Gundawarra's social calendar. More than half the crowd here were out for a rip-roaring night involving loud music, strong drink and an excellent chance of getting up close and personal with the opposite sex.

Whereas Byrne...

Byrne wasn't sure what the hell he was doing here.

'You haven't got cold feet, have you?'

Jane Layton, his best friend's wife, looking fetching in a strapless crimson satin gown, tugged at his elbow.

'Yes,' he admitted. 'I think I have.'

'It's like riding a bike, mate,' coaxed her husband Mitch. 'As soon as you get through the door you'll be cruising, like in the old days.'

Before Byrne could counter this, Jane, used to managing her stubborn husband and three stubborn little boys, took his elbow and firmly steered him to the small porch at the top of the steps.

'Quickly, Mitch,' she said. 'Where's Byrne's disguise?'

Her husband was carrying a voluminous bag, and
now Jane dived into it and produced a mask painted to
represent a black eye-patch and a twinkling blue eye
beneath a wickedly curling black brow.

'You'll make a fabulous pirate, Byrne. You've always
had a touch of danger and glamour about you.' She
offered him an encouraging smile.

But Byrne was beyond the reach of flattery.

'I'm sorry. I don't think I'm ready for this. I've
changed my mind.'

He turned to leave.

A chorus of protests erupted around him. Mitch
grabbed one of his arms, Jane the other. In next to no time,
he was being bustled through a doorway into the already
crowded dance hall, transformed into a pirate by the
mask, a red headscarf and a gold earring in his right ear.

Beside him, Mitch was a masked cowboy, and Jane's
face was obscured by a purple Middle Eastern headdress.

Everyone in the room was wearing a disguise.

Not that the masks hid much, really. Byrne had lived
in this district all his life, and he knew most of the locals
by sight at least. And he could identify most of the re-
vellers even though they were wearing masks and wigs,
and despite the fact that their every day jeans and riding
boots had been replaced by formal dinner suits and
glamorous gowns.

A dancing couple whirled past him, wearing pow-
dered white wigs and glittering Venetian masks, and
Byrne recognised them immediately. The Ropers.

They smiled and called, 'Hi, Byrne.'

So much for being able to stay incognito.

To make matters worse, Mitch and Jane ordered him to have fun and then promptly abandoned him, hurrying to join the crowd on the dance floor.

'Would you like a drink, sir?'

A tray laden with glasses was shoved under his nose by a waiter whose entire head was hidden beneath a green latex Martian mask. Byrne took a beer.

Sipping the frosty ale, he studied the crowd of clowns, jungle creatures, witches and vampires.

'Everyone seems to be having fun,' said a honey-smooth voice beside him.

Byrne turned.

The woman standing next to him was not someone he recognised. She was wearing a shocking pink, curly haired wig and a beautiful mask of azure silk, hand-painted to resemble butterfly wings. By complete contrast to the bright colours on her head, her evening gown was elegant, simple and black, leaving her pale neck and shoulders exposed.

'People do seem to be enjoying themselves,' he agreed.

'But you prefer to watch?'

'Not necessarily. I—er—I'm just getting my bearings.'

She nodded and smiled. 'Never test the depth of the water with both feet.'

He stared at her hard. 'Do I know you?'

Despite his coolness, she smiled again. 'I'm new to the district.'

He let his gaze travel over her. The bright wig hid all trace of her hair. The mask covered two thirds of her face. Her elegant dress hugged a delightfully feminine shape. 'I don't think I recognize you.'

'Does it matter? Isn't the point of this evening to stay in disguise?'

He suppressed a sigh. 'I suppose it is.' After a beat, he added, 'Dangerous, isn't it?'

'Dangerous?' Her head tipped back, and she began to shake with laughter. 'I'm sorry,' she spluttered, struggling to contain her mirth. 'That's just too funny.'

'Why?'

'I never expected to hear a dark and dashing pirate describe a country dance as *dangerous*.'

Byrne found that he was smiling too. 'I'd actually forgotten I'm supposed to be a pirate.'

'Believe me, you look every inch a wicked buccaneer.'

He'd been so busy looking at everyone else that he'd given little thought to how he must appear. Jane Layton's ego-brushing had been water off a duck's back.

But now, with this woman's amused gaze studying him, he felt newly aware of the mask pressing firmly across the bridge of his nose and over his eyes, of the rough cotton cloth clinging to his skull, and the circle of gold clipped to his ear lobe.

Surely no one expected these fragments of costume to transform a conservative cattleman and dour widower into a dangerous, swashbuckling bandit?

What did his friends expect from him this evening? What did this woman expect?

He glanced quickly at her left hand which was holding a glass flute half-filled with sparkling white wine. No rings.

'Are you here alone?'

'I didn't bring a partner. And you?'

'No partner.' He paused. 'We're in the same boat, so I suppose we should introduce ourselves.'

He winced at his lack of finesse. What had happened to the smooth Byrne of old?

But his companion chuckled again and, because most of her face was hidden behind her delicate blue mask, Byrne found himself watching her mouth, which was wonderfully mobile and soft and pink. Her lower lip, even when stretched into a broad grin, was intriguingly, disturbingly lush.

'I don't think introductions are appropriate,' she said. 'The mystery is part of the fun, isn't it?'

Fun? Apart from amusing Riley, fun had been so very low on Byrne's priorities for such a long time that he hardly knew where to start.

Her head tipped sideways as if she were studying him. 'You are planning to have a little fun tonight, aren't you?'

'Well...'

'Oh, come on. What's the point of being here if it's not to have fun?'

'Of course.' He took a deep swig of beer, aware that this was the moment when he should probably ask her to dance. Very soon, she would tire of trying to drag conversation from him and she would drift away to find someone in a better party mood.

And, at the thought of her moving away, he felt an unexpected twinge of disquiet.

'Would you like to dance?' The question almost jumped from his mouth, and he winced again as he heard how terribly nervous he sounded.

For a frantic moment he was a callow, country youth again, heart thumping, palms sweating, petrified of girls.

She said, 'I'd like to dance very much. Thanks.'

She turned, looking for somewhere to place her glass, and for the first time Byrne saw the back of her dress.

He felt as if he'd been struck by lightning.

From the front, her dress had looked quite modest and demure, but its back was virtually non-existent. Two narrow straps of black silk ran from her bare shoulders to a neat bow in the centre of a low waistline.

That was all.

Which left rather a great deal of bare, soft, creamy and feminine skin exposed. Byrne could see, in perfect detail, the neat shape of her pale shoulder blades, the slenderness of her waist and the delicate line of her backbone disappearing enticingly beneath her skirt.

So much skin and so little dress.

When they danced, his hand would… Where on earth…?

Tipping back her head, she finished her wine, set her empty glass down and then turned to him, and her lips, pink and damp with wine, curved into another smile.

Byrne deposited his empty glass and cleared his throat. He felt as if he couldn't breathe.

'OK, let's hit the dance floor.' He managed to sound more confident than he felt, and he held out a hand.

Hell, his hand was trembling.

She placed her hand in his. It was small and cool. He remembered how rough and callused his hands were. Workman's hands. Tessa had never minded.

Tessa. At the thought of his wife, he almost faltered.

But then, thankfully, the band stopped. The dancers slowed to a halt. Byrne released her hand and stood very still, not touching his partner, while the musicians had a brief consultation about the next bracket.

'I need to call you something,' she said, stepping closer in the silence. 'How about Pete? Pirate Pete?'

He smiled. 'That's as good a name as any. What about your name? What are you? Some kind of butterfly?'

'I guess I must be. Do you know the names of any butterflies?'

His right eyebrow lifted. 'Ulysses?'

She shook her head. 'He was a guy.'

'Cairns bird wing? Blue triangle?'

'Bit of a mouthful.'

The music started again. Something loud, fast and snappy.

'Why don't you call me Flutter?' she shouted as she began to sway and tap her feet in time to the music.

'OK. Flutter it is.'

To his relief, the fast music meant they could dance without touching. People around them grinned and waved. Bodies beneath masks jigged and stomped and swung with the beat.

Byrne rather liked the fact that he had no idea who his partner was. Better still, she didn't know him from Adam. Anonymity became his friend.

To his surprise, he picked up the rhythm of the music and he let it pulse through him. Very soon he felt warm and relaxed. The music was upbeat, bright, fun. He began to loosen up, to try a few moves he remembered from years ago.

Flutter grinned and copied him, her curly pink head bobbing in time to the beat, and when the first song flowed into another they danced on, warming to their movements, gathering confidence. He took her hand and spun her around, and saw that arresting vision of her pale back once and then twice.

Like most cattlemen, he had always been fit and well co-ordinated, but he'd forgotten the release that dancing could bring—the unexpected sense of freedom.

Until the music changed tempo and slowed, and couples melted back together, and Flutter drifted closer to Pirate Pete.

For thirty seconds he was ridiculously nervous again, nervous as he took her hand in his, as they inched closer, as he felt her hand rest on his shoulder and caught the faint drift of her perfume. He couldn't bring himself to touch her bare back, so he rested his left hand near her hip.

They began to move slowly in time to the music, their bodies not quite touching. She was slim and lithe in his arms. Her curly pink head skimmed his chin. They were a good fit. Their bodies seemed in tune. No faltering steps.

He wondered if he would have been so at ease if he'd seen her face. Perhaps Jane and Mitch Layton were right. There was something very liberating about masks.

'Hey, Pete.' She lifted her mouth close to his ear. 'You're a good dancer.'

'I'm out of practice.'

'It doesn't show.'

'I think you must be an expert,' he said, remembering that he and Tessa had never danced as easily as this.

'I love dancing. I dance to keep fit.'

He grinned. 'It shows.'

They danced on, and he found himself lost in a crazy fantasy where he took her outside and, without removing her mask, he kissed her. He could almost feel the pliant, lush pressure of her lips against his.

After he kissed her, he would remove her mask and see warmth and desire in her eyes, and —

The music stopped.

'The band will take a break,' someone announced into a microphone.

Couples on the dance floor made their way to the bar.

Byrne asked Flutter, 'Can I get you another drink?'

'Thanks, Pete,' she said. 'I'd love champagne.'

'Wait here. It's too crowded at the bar.'

As he stood in line, he was joined by Mitch in his mask and cowboy hat.

'You look like you're having a good time,' his friend said, grinning madly.

'Yeah. The band's pretty good.'

'So is your partner.' Mitch glanced back to where Flutter stood talking to another woman in red. 'Who is she?'

Byrne shrugged. 'No idea. A butterfly.'

'Sexy dress. Great back.' Mitch, eyeing Flutter's lovely pale skin, grinned.

Byrne merely nodded.

Mitch edged a little closer and lowered his voice. 'Hey, mate, you know what they say about shoulder blades, don't you?'

'No, I don't,' Byrne said dryly, knowing full well that he was being set up for a punchline. 'What do they say?'

'They're the thinking man's breasts.'

Byrne rolled his eyes and forced a light, dismissive laugh, but as he turned to place his order at the bar he felt a bright, embarrassing flash of heat burn the back of his neck.

Fiona was on tenterhooks.

All evening, from the moment she'd seen Byrne Drummond enter the hall, she'd been walking a razor's edge. She'd recognized him immediately. He was such a commanding figure, it would have taken more than a gap of three years and a mask and headscarf to disguise him.

Of course, she wasn't at all surprised that he seemed so familiar. Although she'd only met him once, briefly, in the hospital in that dreadful encounter after the accident, memories—arresting memories—had lingered for three years.

To be honest, the memories hadn't just lingered, they'd taken root inside her. Byrne Drummond had left his imprint on her—and she'd never been quite the same again. Every detail of his rugged, 'lonesome cowboy' appearance had stayed with her. The way he'd stood, shoulders braced and jaw jutting. His deep-set grey eyes, the regal tilt of his head. The firm set of his mouth. The exact size of his hands.

She remembered, too, the deep emotional connection she'd felt, an inappropriate attraction which she'd tried very hard to ignore. And she remembered Byrne's anger—his resentment because of her connection to Jamie. But now, after three long years, she hoped that his anger and grief had been tempered.

Recently, the manager she'd appointed to oversee White Cliffs had resigned, and she'd decided to combine much needed rest and recreation from her high-pressure job with an opportunity to check out the property she hadn't seen for three years.

But there was also a very complicated and exceedingly delicate personal matter that she needed to discuss with Byrne Drummond. She'd set it aside while he was in mourning, but it couldn't be put off for much longer.

'Fiona McLaren, is that you under the butterfly mask?'

Fiona turned to see a purple ball gown topped by a striped bee's mask. Betty Tucker, the ball's chief organizer.

'Yes, it's me,' she said with a laugh. 'But don't tell everyone.'

'Sorry. Are you enjoying yourself, m'dear?'

'I'm having a wonderful time.'

'Lovely.' Betty moved closer and lowered her voice. 'Actually, I have a little favour to ask.'

'How can I help?'

'I thought, because you're a newcomer to the district, that it might be nice if you could award the prizes this evening.'

'Are you sure? I was hoping to stay in the background.'

'No, it's all organized. It'll be a good introduction for you.'

Byrne was returning through the crowd with Fiona's drink.

Betty nodded her head in his direction and smirked. 'Looks like you've already met your neighbour.'

Panic flared mid-centre in Fiona's chest. She needed

to find the right moment to reveal her identity to Byrne, and she did not want Betty to do it for her.

'Don't spoil the surprise, Betty. He hasn't worked out who I am yet.'

'O-o-ooh?'

'Just tell me what I have to do with the prize,' Fiona urged nervously.

'Oh, darling, it's simple.' As Byrne reached them, Betty winked at her and gave a conspiratorial giggle. 'All you have to do is open a couple of envelopes and announce the name of the man and woman with the best masks.'

To Fiona's relief, Betty flashed a beaming smile at both of them and darted away.

Byrne handed her a glass of chilled wine. She took a sip to steady her nerves, and then she smiled at him serenely. 'You'll probably win the prize for the best male mask.'

He made a light, scoffing sound. 'If they choose me, it will only be because they're trying to cheer me up.'

'Do you need cheering up?' she asked, knowing very well that he'd practically been a recluse for the past three years.

'Absolutely,' he said, and he smiled. 'You see? It's your duty to keep me happy tonight, Flutter.'

'My duty? That sounds very old-fashioned. And chauvinistic.'

'We pirates are the old-fashioned, chauvinistic types. You'd better get used to it.'

Used to it. Heavens, what did that mean? Fiona was sure she should be affronted, but for the life of her she couldn't raise any objection to the idea that Byrne might seek more of her company.

His eyes sparkled through the slits in his mask, and his smile warmed her. He sounded happy.

And Fiona felt a pang of guilt. Would he be so relaxed and happy if he knew who she was? Good grief, she'd been crazy to get into this situation. The trouble was, masks encouraged deception. Hiding her identity had seemed an innocent enough game at the start of the evening, but it was beginning to feel more dangerous every minute.

She should stop the charade now.

Taking a deep swig of her wine, she polished off half the glass in one giddying gulp. She'd get this over and done with. She'd tell Byrne who she was.

Now.

Right now.

She opened her mouth to speak. And the band struck up a noisy bracket.

Byrne took a step towards her, and she caught a whiff of his aftershave—fresh and clean, like the ocean. He smiled again and she felt the mysterious power of him ripple over her, as if he'd caressed her. She felt the wine spread through her, warming her veins. Byrne bent his mouth to her ear, and her skin tingled.

'Finish your wine.'

Sinking like a stone beneath his intensely masculine spell, she drained her glass, and then Byrne set it aside and took her hand. And this time he didn't even bother to ask if she'd like to dance. He led her onto the floor and she didn't resist. When he drew her into his arms, his hand skimmed her bare back, and she shivered deliciously.

They danced—close and slow—and within no time at all their bodies were communicating the secret, unmistakeable language of attraction.

They were Pete and Flutter, bound by a mysterious chemistry. How could she destroy that? How could she announce her name now and annihilate a magnetism more thrilling than anything she'd ever felt before?

In the middle of the third song, his mouth dipped close to her ear. 'Would you like to go outside for some fresh air?'

What to say, but yes? Her body was a flashing green light. If he wanted to kiss her, she'd be too weak to say no.

And, as he steered her across the dance floor, she ignored her guilty conscience.

Byrne couldn't quite believe he was leading Flutter through a side door and out into the moonlit shadows. It was the kind of foolish nonsense youngsters engaged in, not staid, single fathers who would never see thirty again.

Perhaps he could blame their masks. He'd been enchanted all evening by Flutter's lips, with only her mouth exposed, so soft and pink and lush. He'd been fantasising about kissing her. Without removing her mask.

Now, she was walking just a little ahead of him, her bare back shimmering palely in the velvet black night.

'You're right,' she said, turning to him. 'It's much cooler and fresher out here.'

Her lips, beneath the azure mask, were moon-washed and pale, and they quivered ever so slightly.

He longed to kiss her. He took her hands in his,

holding her lightly by the fingers. 'I've enjoyed this evening very much.'

'You sound surprised,' she said, smiling.

'I am. Very surprised. I didn't expect to find such charming company.' He let his thumbs rub lazily over her knuckles. 'You're very good company, Flutter.'

An unexpected flush crept up her throat, and he was seized by a desperate urge to trace that burning tide with his lips.

He drew a swift breath. 'I know we haven't met formally, and I hope you don't mind, but I'm going to have to kiss you.'

A tiny sound escaped her—it might have been a gasp or a hiccup or a laugh. But when she lifted her face to him he knew she wanted him.

'I've never been kissed by a pirate.' Her lips parted as she drifted closer.

Fighting a reckless desire to crush her against his roused body, Byrne took her gently in his arms.

He had to take this slowly.

No, he could be wild. She wouldn't mind. She would expect it from a pirate.

No, no. Not wild. A kiss with a stranger in the moonlight should always be romantic.

He slipped his arms around her, and felt her smooth, soft skin beneath his palms. Her curves nestled against him. She was soft and warm and womanly, and his desire mounted so fiercely he could barely breathe. He prayed for restraint as he nudged his lower lip against hers.

Slow, man. Slow. He teased them both mercilessly, with leisurely caresses, letting his mouth trail slowly,

slowly, back and forth over hers. He heard her moan ever so softly, and she began to tremble in his arms. Helpless suddenly, unbearably aroused, he took her face in his hands and kissed her deeply.

His plans for restraint were forgotten and his kiss became fuelled by a fierce hunger. He ravaged her soft mouth with possessive thrusts of his tongue, pulling her hips against him so that she couldn't mistake his need for her.

Had he been drugged? He'd never experienced such need. No kiss had ever felt so dreamlike and yet so real. He was completely lost, crazed by the intoxicating sweetness of her eager mouth. He never wanted this to end.

'Fiona!'

A voice called through the dark, and Flutter went still in his arms.

'Fiona, are you there?'

She stiffened, then pulled away from him. In a daze, he heard her mumble some kind of apology.

'What is it?' he muttered. 'Are they looking for you?'

'Yes,' she whispered. And then, 'I'm sorry.'

Betty, the ball's organizer, was standing in the brightly lit doorway, beckoning. 'Oh, there you are. Can you come now, Fiona? It's time to start giving out the prizes.'

Fiona glanced at Byrne. He was breathing heavily, as if he'd been running, and a dark flush stained his cheekbones. His arms that had held her so tightly hung loose, his big hands empty by his sides.

She felt light-headed and incredibly shaken by his kiss, and needed time to recover. And now, suddenly, she was scared, painfully aware of her deception and the havoc she was about to unleash.

What would Byrne think when he discovered her identity?

'This way. Everyone's waiting,' Betty ordered, her former warmth replaced by a very businesslike and self-important brusqueness.

With a sinking stomach and knocking knees, Fiona followed her, but as she crossed the crowded hall to the stage, now abandoned by the band, she felt as if she was walking a highwire.

Betty Tucker tapped the microphone, and the crowd gathered around. Looking out at the sea of masks, Fiona felt dizzy. She saw Byrne standing in the side doorway, his height and broad shoulders almost filling the space. His mouth was drawn down—a straight un-readable line.

'The committee is giving out prizes for the best dis-guises.' Betty paused to bestow a magnanimous smile on her audience and then, with a grand sweep of her arm, she indicated Fiona. 'And I've asked our newest resident to do the honours. Step right up, Fiona.'

Fiona stepped. But she'd never faced a crowd with less confidence. It would have been preferable at that moment to step right off the end of a pirate's gang plank.

Betty clasped her around the shoulders. 'I'd like you all to meet Fiona McLaren from Sydney, who is taking over the reins at White Cliffs.'

There was a burst of applause and a couple of wolf whistles and Fiona, heart-in-throat, gave a little wave. The figure in the doorway stood still as a mountain.

'Don't be shy now, dear. Take off your wig and mask, so everyone can see who you are.'

Fiona stared helplessly out at the smiling crowd, but it was the one unsmiling man, still standing in the doorway, who bothered her. A man with a carefully guarded heart, who'd let down that guard this evening. Who had trusted her.

She could feel his reproach, feel his scornful gaze burning her. She'd never felt more exposed. If only she could pretend this mask was super-glued to her head. Her hands shook as she began to pull off her wig.

Her long red hair spilled to her shoulders, and the crowd gave an encouraging round of applause. Not wanting to drag the moment out, she whipped off her mask and forced a bright smile.

'And now it's time to hear who our winners are.' Betty handed her two envelopes.

'Right.' Fiona managed to hold her smile and made an amused, throat-clearing sound. 'The winner of the best female mask is...' She slit the first envelope quickly. 'Daisy Oakes.'

There was a thrilled squeal from the back of the hall and a burst of applause as a young woman with a Medusa-like headdress of wriggling rubber snakes came forward.

Once that excitement was over, Fiona looked at the next envelope. 'And now for the best disguised male.' She drew a swift breath and felt a distressing, squirming sensation in her stomach. 'The winner is...'

Please don't let it be Byrne.

Her fingers fumbled and she made a complete hash of

trying to open the envelope. But at last she extracted the small card. 'The—the winner is—Byrne Drummond!'

Fiona's eyes flew to the figure in the doorway. Oh, no. Too late, she realised she'd made a huge mistake.

She could see fury in the tight fists clenched at his sides, in his braced shoulders, in the hard downward curve of his mouth and the belligerent thrust of his jaw.

What a fool she was. By looking straight at him— before he stepped forward—she'd given herself away. Now he knew that all evening she'd been completely aware of his identity, while she'd kept her own a secret.

Without moving from his position in the doorway, he took off his pirate's mask and stared at her, his grey eyes cruelly hard. Unforgiving.

She felt her face collapse with dismay.

Holding her in his grim gaze, he shook his head.

But the hall was full of people applauding. Heads swivelled as many folk turned to grin at Byrne. A couple of people cheered, and then others chimed in. Byrne was a popular choice, even if the prize was rigged.

'Come on up and get your prize, Byrne,' called Betty, beaming broadly.

But Byrne didn't move.

Fiona's heart thundered as he remained where he was in the doorway. Very still, shoulders squared, jaw clenched, back stiff. She caught another outraged flash from his eyes.

A hush fell over the crowd as everyone sensed the sudden tension. And then there were audible gasps of surprise as it dawned on these good folk that the tension was between Byrne and Fiona.

Fiona tried to smile and missed. Her arms lifted out from her sides in an unspoken gesture of entreaty.

Byrne stood perfectly still for another five long seconds, and then spun on his heel and marched out of the hall without a backward glance.

CHAPTER FOUR

HEAD down as he rasped the surface of a pony's hoof, Byrne was locked in dark memories. He'd spent a night disturbed by dreams—dreams he hadn't wanted to remember when he woke.

But when the grey dawn had skulked through the slats in his bedroom shutters he'd remembered not only his inappropriate dreams but everything that had fuelled them. The dancing, the kiss. Fiona McLaren, as attractive, sexy, deceitful and underhanded as her brother.

'Daddy, you're not listening, are you?'

He looked up and blinked. Riley, in her favourite pink ballerina tutu over blue denim jeans, was sitting on the top rail of Brownie's stall, eyeing him crossly.

'Sorry, Scamp. What did you say?'

With an impatient roll of her round, stern eyes, she told him, 'I was asking you an important question.'

His daughter had a penchant for difficult questions: *Daddy, can we get a baby sister? Daddy, what makes the wind blow? Does Mummy still have her birthday up in heaven?*

'What question was that?'

'How many times can you fit Coolaroo on the moon?'

Byrne grinned and shook his head at her as he secured her pony's leg more firmly between his knees. 'Can't work that out now, kiddo. We'd need an encyclopaedia and a calculator.'

Riley pouted and let out a small sigh, but then she folded her plump little arms across her chest and settled against a post to watch in silence. She was a good kid.

A great kid. So grown up at times it frightened him—although at bedtime she still clung to Dunkum and Athengar.

Several times over the last three years, he'd tried to get rid of Athengar, the toy that McLaren woman had brought to the hospital on the day of the accident. But Riley had always been so upset, he'd had to relent.

He knew her attachment to the damn toy was connected in a complicated way to the loss of her mother. She'd lost one and received the other on the very same day. But that interfering, scheming woman should have kept out of their lives.

The rasping complete, he lowered Brownie's hoof and headed for the anvil, just as Ellen Jackson appeared at the door of the stables.

'There's been a phone call for you,' she said. 'From your neighbour, Fiona McLaren.' Ellen was trying hard not to look too impressed by her news.

Byrne scowled. 'What did she want?'

'I'm not sure. She didn't say. I told her you'd ring back.'

'Well, you wasted your breath,' Byrne growled.

* * *

Almost a full day after Byrne's dramatic exit at the Spring Ball, Fiona was still smarting.

It helped that everyone at the ball had assumed Byrne still hadn't recovered from his wife's death and wasn't ready to take centre stage—even at such a light-hearted social event.

But Fiona knew she was the real reason for his behaviour. He was furious that he'd kissed her. And she'd completely wrecked her chances of getting close to him, of winning his confidence and trust.

What a mess. She needed his trust. One hundred percent.

She'd waited three years, giving him time to heal, before she came back to White Cliffs to settle the mystery Jamie had left behind. It was important not to rush, and her plan had been to get to know Byrne better before broaching the delicate subject of paternity.

It wasn't a task she looked forward to. Her life would be much, *much* easier, if she could simply let the matter drop, sweep it under the rug and let Byrne Drummond and Riley carry on with their lives.

She would have dropped it ages ago, would drop it now—in a heartbeat—except for one important thing. If Riley Drummond *was* Jamie's daughter, the child was entitled to her inheritance.

The clause in Jamie's will was something Fiona could not ignore. It was why she was here, why she needed to get close to Byrne.

But what a fool she'd been last night. One look at him, and all she'd done was flirt and flutter. Idiot. So what if she'd have spoiled the magic of the evening by revealing her identity? By remaining silent, she'd spoiled everything else.

She'd been eating her heart out ever since.

She needed a distraction. A walk.

There was a track through the long, heavily timbered paddock that ran from the White Cliffs homestead towards the river. That would do.

It was late afternoon and the air was warm and still, but there was a breeze blowing up from the river and rustling through the tops of the gum trees. As Fiona walked, she disciplined herself to focus on the quiet beauty of the bush, to take note of small details like the drifts of leaves that collected around a fallen log, and the maze of insect tunnels in the log's bark. She listened to the bird calls, and was rather pleased that she recognized the pretty warble of a butcher bird in a tree branch above her.

When she reached the river, she discovered that she was walking along the top of a bluff—a cliff of white limestone. And there was another cliff just as steep on the other side of the river.

White cliffs. How lovely. These must be the landmarks that had given the property its name.

She stopped in the shade of towering ghost gums, overawed by the unexpected grandeur of the twin sheer white walls, and the river below flowing serenely between them. Above the river the sky was a pale blue wash, fading with the last of the day's light, turning pink on its western rim.

It would make a wonderful picnic site—a place tourists would love. She wondered if this was why Jamie had bought the property. When he'd left the airline, he'd been on the lookout for somewhere with tourist potential.

Jamie had often spoken about creating a place where overseas visitors could see the real Australia and meet the colourful characters of the Outback.

Fiona smiled wryly, wondering what the reclusive Byrne Drummond would think of *that*.

There was a sudden movement on the other side of the river. A man on horseback emerged out of the trees on the opposite bank. Sitting straight and proud in the saddle, he rode out onto a wide flat shelf of rock at the top of the cliff and looked down, studying the river valley below.

She recognized him instantly and shivered. Had she only to think of Byrne Drummond to have him suddenly appear?

His face was shadowed by his wide-brimmed hat, but he looked magnificent, silhouetted against the sky—broad-shouldered and long-limbed, astride a magnificent black horse.

Like something out of an old cowboy movie, she told herself. Or commercials she remembered from her childhood. But, despite her efforts to make a joke of Byrne's appearance, she was hypnotised by the sight of him.

Her blood leapt as if an electric current had passed through her. Her insides trembled and turned hollow.

There was no use pretending otherwise—she'd become infatuated by the man.

So silly, given his low opinion of her.

Fiona flinched as she remembered how angry he'd been last night. She wished she understood exactly why. If it had simply been because he hadn't liked being deceived, she could perhaps soothe him with a grovelling apology.

Or was there more behind his anger? What did Byrne know about Riley's paternity?

One thing was certain—the task of raising that delicate subject would be a hundred times harder now.

At least they were separated by a river. She wasn't ready for another confrontation.

The tension in her shoulders eased as Byrne started to turn his horse back into the trees, but he suddenly stiffened and glanced back across the river.

He swivelled in the saddle to take a harder look. His horse danced beneath him, taking impatient sidesteps, but Byrne's gaze remained fixed. On Fiona.

She took a deep breath and waved to him, forcing a smile in spite of her slamming heartbeats. His response was to urge the horse into a sudden canter.

But, instead of heading for the trees, he took off along the top of the cliff till he reached a track cut into the rocky wall of the riverbank, and without the slightest hesitation he began to steer his horse down the dangerously steep track.

Surface gravel, loosened by the horse's hooves, sprayed over the edge and into the river bed below. Fiona watched, her heart in her mouth, almost certain that Byrne was risking his neck. And equally certain he was planning to cross the river, to confront her.

Here. Alone in the bush.

How foolish of her to have assumed that a wide river would serve as a moat.

In no time he reached the bottom and disappeared

from her view, but she could hear splashing and the rattle of water-smoothed stones beneath the horse's hooves. And then silence, followed by the heavy thud and clop of hooves on the worn track as he ascended the cliff on her side.

When he appeared at the cliff top, she felt a jolt deep inside her, and fine tremors whispered over her skin. It was ridiculous, but she couldn't help it. This man stirred her senses as no man ever had.

He brought the horse to a halt and looked down at her.

'Hello, Byrne.'

He frowned darkly. 'Why have you come here?'

So, not a word about last night.

As if the dancing and the kiss had never happened.

Damn the man. The cheek of him. This was her land. She had every right to be here.

'I could ask you the same question, Mr Drummond. You're on my property, you know.' More confident now, she lifted her chin defiantly. 'I'm sorry, but if you expect me to join you in neighbourly conversation you're going to have to get down off your high horse.'

His right eyebrow lifted and his eyes pierced her with a sharp, sparkling glance that might—just *might*—have carried a glimmer of amusement. Or maybe it was plain and simple anger. Before she could be certain, the fleeting emotion vanished and his face was impassive and cool again.

Nevertheless, he did as she asked. Swinging his leg over the saddle in one easy, fluid motion, he dismounted and stood before her, holding his horse's reins lightly in one hand.

The horse seemed enormous to Fiona. It snorted and bared its teeth at her, and she took a quick step back.

'He won't bite.'

'I'm glad to hear it,' she said with as much dignity as she could muster, but she didn't sound quite as brave as she would have liked. Not with Byrne standing close, almost touching.

It was so hard to carry on as if last night had never happened. She could remember so clearly how it had felt to have this man's arms around her, to have his mouth intimately locked with hers and his roused body thrust urgently against her.

She wiped her damp palms on her jeans. 'I take it you're not pleased to see me.'

He stared at her grimly. 'What brought you back here?'

'Haven't you heard? I lost my manager. He was head-hunted by Pastoral Pacific.'

'No, I hadn't heard that. You don't plan to settle here, do you?'

'And what if I do? Why would you object?'

He took far too long to answer. Finally, with his jaw thrust at a stubborn angle, he said, 'What do you know about this place? How much stock do you carry?'

Fiona gasped. 'What is this, Byrne? An examination? You want me to prove that I'm fit to be your neighbour?'

He lifted one massive shoulder in an offhand shrug. 'Neighbours out here usually know how to manage a cattle property.'

'Implying what, exactly?' Fiona was so tense she was shaking.

'Exactly?' His eyes shimmered. 'Well, they know exactly how much stock they have. Exactly what condition the stock's in. Exactly where the cattle are on their property. They know when they need to muster and how they're going to do it.'

If he hadn't been standing right next to his horse, she might have punched him square on his arrogant nose. She'd confronted males like him before—on every rung of her way up the corporate ladder. She could handle Byrne Drummond, Esquire.

Drawing a deep breath and letting it out slowly, she answered with exaggerated patience. 'OK, Mr Drummond, how's this? I have three thousand, four hundred and twenty six head of cattle. They've been vaccinated against tick fever, leptospirosis and vibriosis. Every beast has access to sufficient feed and water, so I'd say they're in fine condition. I plan to muster before Easter next year, or as soon as the wet season's over, whichever comes first. And I'll use contract musterers. I have an excellent list of contacts.'

The surprise in his eyes was very gratifying, and Fiona was grateful that she'd taken time to study the detailed stock report that Bart Jones had left for her.

And now, she decided, was an appropriate moment to change tactics, while Byrne was on the back foot. Adopting a tone of appeasement, the one she used when soothing the ruffled feathers of agitated board members, she said, 'Byrne, we both lost people we love in that terrible accident three years ago. But it wasn't my fault. I think you've carried a grudge against me for long enough. Just remember, I am not my brother's keeper.'

He stared hard at something on the far side of the river, rubbed his hand over his stubbled jaw. 'I still think you'd be crazy to try to take this place on.'

She sighed. 'Because I'm a woman?'

The briefest of smiles tipped the corners of his mouth, but then he shook his head. 'Because you don't have any practical knowledge of the cattle industry.'

'A cattle property is a business, isn't it? I know a great deal about business.'

At that very moment, her mobile phone rang.

'Excuse me.' She extracted the phone from the pocket of her jeans. It was her PA's number, and she shot Byrne a wry smile. 'A business matter.' Into the phone, she said, 'Hi, Sam, how can I help you?'

'Fiona, I'm sorry to bother you again, but there's a new Sydney advertising agency about to launch, and they really want to pitch to you for our company's business.'

'Who are they?'

'A mega-trendy, upmarket group called Shazam.'

'Ah, yes.' Fiona nodded. 'I know who's behind this. I thought they might surface again. Tell them we have a long-standing contract with Jefferson's. Started with a handshake twenty years ago, and we're not about to jump ship. Let them pitch, but Michael will have to handle it. Tell him they will have to be sensational before we give them anything, even small jobs. And warn him not to associate with anyone who worked for Alpha Promotions before they were closed down by the fraud squad.'

She disconnected and, slipping the phone back into her pocket, looked up to see Byrne watching her with a slow, sceptical smile.

'Where were we?' she asked him.

'You were telling me how good you are at business,' he said dryly. 'And I was about to remind you that you know nothing about *this* business.'

'Oh, come on, Byrne, give me a break. I'm smart. I can learn how to manage cattle. It's not a secret black art.'

But even as she said this she knew snapping at a man like Byrne would only make him more stubborn, so she back-pedalled again.

Resisting the impulse to sigh, she said, 'At ease, Byrne. You're not in danger. I won't be a long-term neighbour. If you really want to know, I'm here because I plan to sell White Cliffs.'

She expected him to be pleased, was surprised that he looked startled. He frowned and dropped his gaze to the reins in his hand, and flicked the soft leather against his fingers.

'You must be happy about that.'

His head jerked up. His cool grey eyes held hers, as if he was trying to take her measure, and then his gaze warmed and he smiled—a proper eye-crinkling, cheek-creasing smile.

'Of course I'm pleased,' he said. 'I'm delighted you're moving on. You've made a sensible business decision.'

She swallowed the unreasonable hurt that ploughed deep in her chest.

'Actually,' Byrne continued, 'I'd like to make you an offer.'

'To buy White Cliffs?' She tried to sound unperturbed and failed.

'I've been looking for an opportunity to expand. It would make good business sense.'

But there's every chance that half of it already belongs to your daughter.

Fiona struggled, really struggled, to remain composed. Byrne's willingness to make this purchase had caught her completely off guard. If she wasn't careful, he'd secure White Cliffs and she'd be packed up and heading back to Sydney—and not one step nearer to her goal.

She had to find out the truth about Riley's relationship to Jamie.

Byrne's eyes narrowed cautiously. 'What's the matter? I'm prepared to offer you a fair price.'

The sun was starting its downhill slide to the horizon, taking the day's warmth with it. Fiona rubbed at her arms, while her mind hunted frantically for a way to stall him. 'I—I wasn't planning to sell straight away. I've taken leave, and I'm having a bit of a holiday. And—and the property's not ready.'

'You want to make improvements?'

'Yes.' She was grasping at straws now. 'I want to—to renovate—the homestead.'

'The homestead?' His shocked exclamation startled his horse, making it snort and skitter sideways, hooves striking the ground noisily.

A scared cry broke from Fiona as she scrambled several steps back, adding to the horse's nervousness. Its head jerked, almost hauling the reins from Byrne's hand.

'What's the matter with him?' she cried, ready to run for her life.

'He's a little tense.' Byrne soothed the stallion with a gentle word as he stroked its nose. Then he glanced her way and saw that she was shaking. 'Are you frightened of animals?'

'No.' Then after a beat, 'Well—not all animals.'

He grinned. 'Just the ones with hooves.'

'The ones ten times my size.'

She watched Byrne's long fingers calmly caress the horse, and remembered how those fingers had felt when they had touched her skin, and she felt unaccountably miserable. And very much a city woman out of her depth.

Eager to change the subject, she said, 'Why shouldn't I renovate the homestead?'

'Cattle investors won't be looking for a fancy house.'

'But their wives might be.' When he looked as if he planned to protest, she hurried on. 'It's high time men in the Outback paid their women more consideration.'

He let out a harsh, disparaging sound. 'You'd be better off looking after your boundaries. Your manager wasn't quite as efficient as he seemed; your fences and fire breaks are in a bad way.'

'Oh, are they really?' Fiona cast a hasty glance into the bush, wondering where the fire breaks were. 'Right,' she said. 'Thanks for the heads up. I'll have someone check those things out, too.'

He turned back to his horse, examined one of its straps, and then he looked back at her. 'You were trying to ring me this morning. Why?'

It was the last question she'd expected. Flustered, she stammered, 'It—it doesn't matter. It's not important now.'

His eyes signalled clearly that he didn't believe her. With his hand on the pommel as if he was about to remount, he stood very still, watching her. Waiting.

She thought how incredibly handsome he looked with his horse beside him and the ruddy sunset behind him—like some kind of mythical hero.

She felt the memory of his kiss seep into her bones—his lips and tongue ravishing her.

It was irrational, it was naïve and harum-scarum, but all she wanted now was to throw herself at this gorgeous man.

Forget Jamie. Forget the terrible burden he'd left behind.

She wanted to tell Byrne she'd fallen helplessly in lust with him. Beg him shamelessly for more of those kisses.

The urge was so violent, it shocked her. Never had she felt so out of control, so overpowered by longing that she could hardly think straight.

But she had to think. Byrne was offering her a chance to explain about the ball, to set things right between them.

Drawing a deep, steadying breath, she said carefully, 'I was ringing to apologise about last night. I was going to try to explain. You see, I didn't set out to deceive you. It—it just sort of happened. I was having such a good time. You were wonderful company, Byrne. And—and I didn't want to spoil the fun.'

His face was a blank mask as he listened to this, but then he smiled suddenly and so beautifully that Fiona felt the warmth of it flood through her, making her blood leap.

'Apology accepted,' he said quietly.

Good heavens. A truce.

And then, to her further astonishment, he said, 'It *was* fun, wasn't it?'

And he raked her with a bright gaze that stirred her unbearably.

The twilight closed in around them. The horse stamped its feet.

Byrne looked away to the darkening sky. 'Sun will set soon.' He threw the reins over the horse's head.

She had no idea when she would see him again, and she wished she had a reasonable excuse to detain him.

'How's Riley?' she asked.

He set the toe of his boot into the stirrup. 'She's fine.'

'Is she going to school yet?'

'Yes.' He swung up into the saddle and looked down at her from what seemed like an enormous height. 'She started school this year. Proving to be quite a bright little button.'

It was impossible to miss the glow of pride in his eyes.

'I guess she must have grown a lot.'

'Sure has. She's six now. Six going on sixteen.'

The horse was restless beneath him, its tail swishing impatiently.

She knew he would want to make the journey home before dark, so she let him go with a careless wave. 'I might see you around some time.'

'Let me know if you have any problems getting help with the fences or the fire breaks.'

'I will. Thank you.'

He turned the horse's head and cantered to the edge of the cliff.

Not even a goodbye. She chewed her lips and tried to tell herself that she didn't care.

But suddenly Byrne wheeled his horse in a tight about face and sent her a smile, a gorgeous, shy grin. Raising his right hand, he tipped the front of his Akubra hat.

'Have a good evening, Fiona.'

She felt as tingly inside as a schoolgirl.

In bed later that evening, with her pillows piled comfortably, nursing a fat mug of hot chocolate, Fiona gave herself a stern lecture. Byrne Drummond was off limits.

She had to be sensible—put him out of her mind. Falling for him wasn't an option. He wanted her off the property as soon as possible.

Maybe there'd been a vibe or two down there on the river bank.

But any vibes she'd felt had been the vibes of a man suddenly sensing the opportunity for a short-term encounter. And this situation was far too complex to even consider it.

She forced her thoughts in the direction of home renovations instead. Settling back against the nest of pillows, she let an entire restoration of the homestead unfold in her imagination.

She would paint this place inside and out. Something tasteful and pretty—pale, restful colours. She'd rip up the dusty old carpets and tattered linoleum, and restore the original timber floors to highly polished beauty. There would be a new bathroom and a properly fitted kitchen.

What a pity she couldn't furnish the house, too. It would look fabulous filled with antique furniture—a big, scrubbed pine table and dresser in the kitchen, shelves crammed with bottled preserves. An elegant dining setting and a sideboard with a mirror reflecting a cut-glass vase filled with wildflowers. Beds covered in sumptuous, plump quilts in a patchwork of ginghams and floral prints.

She'd never restored an old house before, but the challenge excited her. She would be in her element, on the phone and the internet, liaising with interior designers, architects, builders, painters and hardware stores.

And the best thing about it was that the renovations would give her the perfect excuse to stay in the district for a couple of months. Surely in that time she would find an opportunity to speak to Byrne?

She winced as a sharp, scorching pain speared her chest.

Heartburn had been bothering her for weeks now. Setting her mug on the bedside table, she got up and stretched, trying to open her chest and release the pressure. She walked to the window and took a deep breath.

Outside, the stars were covered by clouds and the night was black as pitch.

'How long will I have to keep putting this off?' she asked aloud.

For three years she'd remained silent about her discovery of Jamie's possible links with the Drummond family. Her secret felt like an axe hanging over her head, and the stress of it was playing havoc with her insides.

Horrible as it was going to be, she had to tell Byrne what she knew. Soon. If she put it off much longer, she might make herself really ill.

In her business she'd seen too many good people go down with stress related illnesses. She'd been proud of her own stress management, and she knew she had to unburden herself as soon as possible.

But when?

Would there ever be a right moment?

This afternoon Byrne had forgiven her for the deception at the ball, and he'd actually started to trust her again. It felt good. His approval mattered to her. A lot. Too much.

Way too much.

A soft groan of despair broke from her as she walked back to the bed. She took a cautious sip of the warm chocolate.

There was only one way to approach this. She had to concentrate on the good that would come from it. If Riley *was* Jamie's daughter, she should receive the inheritance she was entitled to.

It was for that reason alone that Fiona had to raise the dreaded subject with Byrne. And she had to do it soon. For Riley's sake. She had to face Byrne's anger, and she had to discuss this painful subject even though she knew it would shatter his trust and almost certainly break his heart.

And her heart, too—because once this was out in the open he would hate her. For ever.

CHAPTER FIVE

'How old is Gran, Daddy?'

Riley tugged at Byrne's hand as they surveyed the stand of birthday cards in the Gundawarra newsagency.

'Is she one hundred?'

Byrne chuckled. 'Nowhere near one hundred.'

He chuckled again, imagining his sixty-four-year-old mother's reaction if she'd overheard her granddaughter's question.

He looked down at Riley now, in her green school uniform, bouncing beside him like a gleeful grasshopper. Her excitement had begun as soon as she'd come out of school and had seen his utility truck parked by the fence. Her nut-brown eyes beneath her straight brown fringe had shone like summer stars—simply because he'd come into town to collect her from school so that together they could celebrate Gran's birthday.

Family. What would he do without them?

'What about this one?' Riley seized a card sporting a picture of an elderly woman performing an astonishing acrobatic feat and, with a delighted giggle, she handed it to him.

Byrne opened it. And encountered a bawdy reference to sex in the message inside. 'I'm afraid Gran wouldn't want this one.'

'Why not?' His daughter challenged him with a little scowl and a pouting lower lip. 'The old lady on the front is just like Gran, and she looks like she's having fun.'

He pointed to a charming card with pink lace and roses. 'I'm sure Gran would rather have something like this, Scamp. Something elegant.'

She glanced at it, unimpressed. Her eyes drifted to a row of humorous cards with cartoon characters, and she picked up one with cheerful black and white cows on the cover.

Byrne checked the inside message. More sexual innuendos.

'This is the one she'd like,' he insisted, opening the demure pink one and discovering an appropriately sentimental poem inside. 'We can buy pink ribbons to match for the present.'

Riley pulled a face. 'Gran doesn't like pink much.'

'Of course she does. Women always like pink.'

'No they don't.'

Coming from a daughter obsessed with every shade from pastel pink to fuchsia, Byrne found this resistance confusing. 'But you love pink.'

'I know I do. But Gran doesn't.'

'How do you know?'

'She told me.'

'Are you sure?'

She nodded emphatically. 'Haven't you noticed

anything, Daddy? Gran hardly has any pink things in her house. She has lots of yellow stuff. Yellow and blue.'

Byrne had to admit he'd never taken much notice of his mother's interior decor, but now he made an effort to recall dinnerware, sofas and cushions, and he realized the kid was right. Yellow and blue. And lots of white. How about that? Were all females born with an innate awareness of these things?

'What about this card, then?' he said. 'Do you think she'd like dais—'

He broke off as a woman stepped out from behind a corner display and almost collided with him.

'Sorry,' she said, with a cheery smile. And then, as they recognized each other, her smile faded and she looked startled and flushed in the cheeks. 'Byrne.'

Fiona McLaren.

Her hair was tied up into some kind of casual, loose knot, and she was wearing faded jeans and a plain white T-shirt. Such simple, everyday clothes should have made her look ordinary, but they seemed to accentuate the fiery richness of her hair, the delicacy of her cheek-bones and the lithe trimness of her body.

The unexpected sight of her affected Byrne in ways that it shouldn't. He drew a swift breath to relieve the sudden tightness in his throat—and elsewhere. 'Good afternoon, Fiona.'

She seemed ill at ease, which was unusual for her. Her green eyes shimmered, and she began to fiddle ner-vously with the magazines she held.

'I decided to buy these for inspiration,' she said, as if she needed to justify why she was there. 'For the renovations.' She lowered the magazines a little so he could see the covers—glossy photos of country-style kitchens and bathrooms.

Then she looked down at the small figure beside him, and her eyes seemed to grow huge, her face pale. 'This must be Riley.'

Byrne nodded. 'Fiona is our new neighbour,' he explained to his daughter.

'Hello.' The little girl offered a smile, but she was shy with strange grown-ups, and she slipped her hand inside his. He gave her warm little fingers a reassuring squeeze.

He said, 'As you can see, Riley's growing faster than grass in the wet season.'

'Yes.' This was uttered in a kind of strangled whisper.

Weird, Byrne thought. Fiona was looking strangely upset, hugging her magazines tightly against her chest, her eyes devouring Riley and looking more and more miserable.

'So you two are shopping together, are you?'

'It's my Gran's birthday,' Riley announced importantly.

If possible, Fiona looked even more upset. She couldn't take her eyes from the child. 'Your gran lives here? In Gundawarra?'

Riley nodded eagerly, making her ponytails bounce.

'Directly behind the Post Office,' added Byrne.

Fiona produced a smile with obvious difficulty. 'That's nice. Very handy.'

She dropped her gaze to their clasped hands, and he was sure he saw a suspicious silver sparkle.

What the heck was the matter with her?

There was nothing about his innocent six-year-old daughter that would upset a stranger like Fiona McLaren.

Unless...

Unless she was remembering the last time the three of them had met. In the hospital three years ago. When she'd brought that toy, Athengar. And when Byrne, broken with grief, had been so damn angry with her.

But he couldn't believe Fiona would still be upset about that. She wasn't the super-sensitive type. She'd been totally confident and relaxed at the ball. And yesterday, when he'd been downright rude to her, she'd taken his insults on the chin and then come out of her corner fighting.

'Daddy.' Riley gave his hand an impatient tug. 'Gran's waiting for us.'

'Yes, we'd better get going.' Byrne looked again at the card he'd selected. Daisies with smiley faces in their bright yellow centres. He sent Fiona a swift grin. 'My daughter's just taught me something new. Apparently, not all women like pink. My mother in particular.'

Fiona smiled wryly. 'A perceptive head on young shoulders.'

He showed the daisy card to Riley. 'This should do, shouldn't it?'

She grinned, and skipped beside him. 'Yep. Gran will *love* that one.'

'And this ribbon,' he said, snagging an elaborate yellow satin bow.

'I'll leave you to it.' Fiona backed away from them.

'Yeah, sure. See you around.' And then, just before she turned away, he surprised himself. 'Actually, I might drop over some time and show you where the problems are with your fences. They need fixing, or you'll lose cattle.'

'That would be good. Thanks.'

As she smiled, she looked into his eyes, and Byrne felt a tumbling sensation in his chest.

''Bye Riley. I hope your gran likes her birthday card.'

''Bye.'

He watched Fiona hurry to the front of the shop to pay for her magazines. One thing was certain, she was damn easy on the eye, one of those neatly made women who did everything gracefully, even searching in a wallet for coins. Watching her, it was easy to ignore the gut-level warning that told him Fiona McLaren was trouble.

How could she do it?

Fiona spent another sleepless night, tossing and turning while her heart and her head played tug of war.

How on earth could she raise the subject of paternity with Byrne Drummond?

He adored his little girl. They were so close, great mates. A little team. It was a crazy idea to try to dig up the truth. Too cruel.

Her heart recoiled from the thought of causing pain and hurt. She should stay silent about this and walk away, go back to her life in the city and leave the Drummonds unscathed.

But her head provided arguments just as forceful, stubbornly analysing the situation from every point of view, reasoning that there was more than a father's tender feelings at stake here. There was a little girl's future, her financial security. Riley was entitled to her share of White Cliffs.

If Byrne married again and had sons, they might take over Coolaroo when they were older, and Riley could find herself out on a limb. Girls and women needed money of their own.

Fiona believed this fervently. Her own father had died when she was seven. He hadn't bothered with life insurance, and her mother hadn't had the confidence to try to get a job—so she'd struggled to raise Fiona and Jamie on a meagre widow's pension.

The gloom of poverty had soured their mother's smile and cast a mean shadow over their childhood, and as soon as they were old enough both Jamie and Fiona had worked as hard as they could to achieve financial independence. It was why Fiona was so focused on her career. Why, at the age of thirty three, she owned a trendy apartment in downtown Sydney and another in the suburbs that she rented out, as well as a solid investment portfolio.

Security was everything.

If she couldn't be a proper aunt for Riley, she wanted to at least ensure that the girl got the money she was entitled to.

There was always the option of just letting it go, and then leaving the money from White Cliffs to Riley in her will.

But when would that be?

She tried to picture that time in the dim, distant future. She would almost certainly be a lonely and child-less old spinster, and little Riley would be a middle-aged matron. Riley could inherit everything, the money that had been invested from the sale of White Cliffs and the significant money Fiona had made.

But how terrible it could be for Riley, at fifty or so, to discover her true father's identity. The shockwaves and repercussions for her and her family could be horrendous.

Surely it was better to bring the whole thing into the open now, to face up to Byrne, ask for a DNA test, and determine once and for all whether Riley was Jamie's daughter?

An inner voice whispered: *better for whom?*

Certainly not for Byrne.

Groaning, she slumped back onto the bed. What a terrible mess her brother had left behind.

She was haunting his dreams.

Sitting on the top step with his back against a verandah post, Byrne stared out into the bush, hoping to clear his head of the dreams that had disturbed him.

He watched the sky, the spread of stars and the solitary moon, almost full and gleaming palely through the tops of the gum trees. And he saw Fiona McLaren's pale face and the faint dusting of freckles that danced across her skin.

He grinned at the thought of those freckles. He couldn't think why he hadn't noticed them at the ball. Perhaps because she was wearing a mask and make-up. But yesterday, down at the river, and again today in town, her skin had been totally clear and natural and he'd discovered freckles.

Tiny golden-brown freckles, on her nose and her

cheeks and her chin. And on her neck, too, disappearing into the V of her blouse. And her lips. How sexy was that? Tiny, intriguing, delightful pinpricks on her smooth soft skin, begging to be tasted.

He'd been undone when he'd seen them. It was crazy, but those freckles, along with the sparkling light of battle in her green eyes, had wiped away the urge to wage war with Fiona, even though she was Jamie McLaren's sister.

She wasn't a Hollywood beauty. But she was certainly attractive, with an earthiness that he couldn't get out of his mind. She had a way of looking at him, a message in her eyes, an unmistakeable signal that made hot blood pound through his loins.

And she was one hell of a kisser.

Which brought him back to his dreams. And why he was out here at one in the morning, asking himself if Tessa would mind if he became interested in another woman.

They hadn't talked about it, had been too young to contemplate death. But he knew deep down that, if he'd been the one killed, Tessa would have found another man. It was the way she'd been. There'd been a string of boyfriends before she married him. Including McLaren.

Byrne sighed.

Best not to let his mind go down that torturous route. Asking questions about why an old flame like McLaren had moved to White Cliffs had driven him crazy for too long.

It had taken a long time to let go of the past and everything he'd lost. And he needed to look to the future now. He had Riley, Coolaroo and possibly White Cliffs, if he was lucky.

And an intriguing, freckled redhead next door.

Perhaps it was time he got a little more neighbourly.

By mid-morning, Fiona was no closer to a decision when she heard the grumble of a vehicle coming up the dirt track to the homestead.

She hurried to the kitchen window, and saw a Land Cruiser pulling to a stop near the front steps.

Byrne Drummond emerged, and stood beside his vehicle with his thumbs hitched in the belt loops of his jeans while he looked about him—at the homestead with its peeling paint and sagging windows, and at the straggling garden with its unkempt rose bushes and drooping poinsettias struggling for survival among rampant weeds.

Painful heartburn spiked in the middle of her chest. He was here. And she had to find the courage to speak to him this morning.

She couldn't put this off any longer. She had to do it now. Get it out in the open. No turning back.

But she didn't rush to the door. She stayed at the window, watching him, gathering strength for what she had to do.

When he'd apparently seen enough, he mounted the front steps with a jaunty spring in his step and an optimistic rat-a-tat on her door.

His smile, when she opened the door, was so unexpectedly warm and impossibly gorgeous she felt her heart sliding away into a spiralling pulse.

Not a good start.

'Hi, neighbour,' he said.

'Good morning, Byrne.'

He glanced down at flakes of old paint that had stuck to his knuckles when he'd knocked, and he grinned. 'I take back what I said about the renovations. You're right. This place could do with a spruce up.'

'It's in pretty bad shape, isn't it?'

He nodded and smiled again, and Fiona wished he'd stuck to scowling. Smiles made her task a whole lot harder.

'I was passing this way and thought I'd follow up on my promise to clue you in about your fence lines.'

'Oh, right. Thank you. Would you like to come inside?'

He stayed on the doorstep. 'How busy are you?'

'Not very. I've been on the phone, sweet-talking painters and builders into coming out here to give me a quote.'

'Any luck?'

'Some.' Then after a beat, 'What did you have in mind?'

'I thought, if you weren't in the middle of anything too important, you might be able to come with me now in the Land Cruiser. I could take you over to the eastern boundary and show you the trouble spots with your fences.'

'Oh, all right. Let me grab my shoes.'

His gaze dropped to her bare feet, complete with baby-pink toenail polish, and his face broke into a grin. 'By all means.'

Fiona's stomach pitched. Why did Byrne have to become so super-friendly all of a sudden? Why today, when she'd finally resolved to tell him the one thing that would obliterate that sexy grin?

Halfway across the shabby living-room carpet to

fetch her shoes, she stopped. She couldn't jump into Byrne's car and ride around the property with him. She couldn't allow him to give up his time to be neighbourly and helpful, and then drop her bombshell.

It had to be now. Now or never.

She looked back across the room to where he waited on the doorstep. Sunlight was streaming through the leaves of an overhanging gum tree, high-lighting the glossy sheen of his dark hair and the way his shoulders stretched the pale blue cotton of his shirt, the tan on his face, the flash of his teeth as he smiled at her.

And she almost cried aloud with panic.

She swallowed a prickly lump in her throat, and her chest burned.

'Actually,' she said. 'If you don't mind, Byrne, there's something I need to talk to you about first.'

'Sure,' he said easily. 'What is it?'

Sweat filmed her upper lip as she gestured for him to enter. 'Come in and take a seat.'

He frowned, but didn't refuse.

The room seemed smaller when he entered. 'Can I get you something? Would you like tea or coffee?'

He shook his head. 'I don't need anything.'

'This chair is surprisingly comfortable.' She pointed to a rather faded and worn armchair.

Byrne sat, still frowning, and she guessed he'd picked up on her nervousness. But he looked relaxed enough as he eased himself back into the deep chair and crossed an ankle over a knee.

She noticed that his riding boots were polished and

his jeans and shirt pressed. He'd made an effort before he'd come here, as if he wanted to make a good impression. Oh, help. Could this get any worse?

Byrne's head tipped to one side as he studied her. 'So, what's the problem, Fiona?'

Perched on the edge of a chair opposite him, she wished this was simply a tricky interview with a difficult client; she was an expert in handling delicate business matters. But matters of the heart were way beyond her expertise.

Now, she hoped he couldn't see her hand shaking as she reached for the folder on the coffee table and set it in her lap. She took a deep breath and tucked a stray wing of hair behind her ear. As if tidiness would help. Nothing was going to help her.

'I'm sorry, Byrne, but what I have to say is terribly difficult. If there was a way I could forget it or ignore it, I would.'

She had his full and earnest attention now. The relaxed attitude evaporated. He sat straight, both feet on the floor, his hands fisted on the chair's arms, eyes alert and steel-sharp.

Fiona fingered the edges of the folder. 'I found something, when I was going through my brother's things after the accident. Something that has rather disturbed me.' She paused, and then said very quickly, 'It seems that he knew your wife, Tessa.'

His eyes flashed warily. 'Yes. What of it?'

'You knew that?'

'Of course. We didn't have secrets. Tessa and your brother were friends before we were married.'

'You're aware they were an item?'

'Yes. For a time,' he said stiffly. 'What's your point, Fiona?'

Disconcerted, she looked down, needing a moment to come to terms with this. Somehow she hadn't expected Byrne to know about his wife's history with Jamie. Did he know everything? Was she about to make a huge fool of herself?

'What's this about?' Byrne demanded.

The dreaded moment.

She opened the folder and the three photos were there, just as they'd been when she'd found them three years ago. 'I found these, Byrne. I—I'm not sure what they mean, exactly, but I thought I should show them to you.'

Closing it again, she leaned forward, holding the folder out.

Byrne didn't move. He stared at her trembling hand, his expression so grim and his face so stony that it might have been hewn from granite.

'Why don't you just spit it out? What are these photos? What are you trying, so inadequately, to tell me?'

Oh, help. He wasn't going to give her any leeway here.

'There are three photos, Byrne. I don't know why Jamie left them like this, in this folder, singled out. I couldn't find any explanation, so I had to ask myself why. And—and the only conclusion I could come to was that he believed…'

The walls of her throat seemed to stick together, and she had to swallow. Twice.

Byrne waited, watching with fierce attention.

'I—I suspect that Jamie believed he was Riley's father.'

Oh, God. It was out. Fiona's face burst into flames. Through a sheen of tears, she saw Byrne's reaction.

Stunned shock. Horror.

He shot to his feet and stood, staring at her, his eyes dark and glassy with agonised disbelief, the way he'd looked that first time, on the day of the accident.

And then, after long, horrible seconds, there was hatred, too—directed straight at her. He hated her for inflicting this mortal blow.

He glared at the folder in her hand. 'Give them to me.'

She stood, and he snatched the folder roughly from her. Turning, he strode across the room to a desk in the corner. With his back to her, he set the folder down and opened it.

Fighting tears, Fiona remained in the middle of the room, watching the tension in Byrne's suntanned neck.

'The first photo of the little girl on the beach is my mother,' she said to his back.

The clock on the wall ticked, and the ceiling fan circled above them with a swish-swish-creak. Outside, a crow squawked. Apart from these sounds, and the thumping of her heart, there was deathly silence.

She watched as Byrne slowly studied each photograph, as he picked them up one by one and turned them over to read the inscriptions on the back. He seemed to take for ever, and Fiona thought she might expire from the tension. She couldn't see the expression on his face, but she felt the horrific impact of each discovery.

Her mother, looking so much like Riley.

Jamie and Tessa, arm in arm.

Sweet, innocent Riley.

Hammer blows pounding, crushing, destroying.

An awful sound, a kind of dry, keening moan, broke from him, and Fiona shoved her hand hard over her lips to stifle a sob. She couldn't bear this.

Until this moment, she'd nursed a tiny hope that Byrne would take one look at these photos and toss them aside, laughing while he told her that what she was trying to suggest was impossible, that he knew without any shadow of a doubt that Riley was his flesh and blood.

But no.

Byrne pressed a fist against his mouth and drew a sharp, choked breath, and she knew he was struggling to suppress a desperate need to break down.

'Byrne, I am so, so sorry,' she said, taking a tentative step towards him.

He whirled on her, blocking her with an outstretched hand, his face florid with a thousand emotions. 'Stop. I don't want to hear a word from you. Not a word.'

He began to tremble, and his jaw clenched tightly as if that would stop it. The colour drained from his skin as he fought for control. It seemed an age, but perhaps it was only a second or two later, when he strode across the room to the front doorway and stood on the step looking out, his hands braced on his hips, his back rigid, shoulders squared, as if readying himself for more blows.

Fiona didn't dare to move or make a sound.

Byrne stayed there for ages, staring off into the bush, and after a bit, because she couldn't stand there watching him and she couldn't think what else to do, she went into the kitchen and put the kettle on.

Her heart was breaking for Byrne. She kept picturing him as he'd been yesterday with Riley in the newsagent's—father and his daughter, a close and happy team, selecting his mother's birthday card.

Why in God's name had it ever seemed right to do this to them?

The electric kettle came to the boil, billowed steam and then switched itself off, but she ignored it as tears coursed down her cheeks.

And then, in the next room, footsteps sounded. Byrne was coming back into the house, and she quickly swiped at her tears with the backs of her hands and hurried to the entrance to the living room.

'What game have you been playing?' he demanded through gritted teeth.

'Game?' she whispered. 'I don't know what you mean.'

'You kept these photos to yourself for three years. I suppose they were your amusing little secret. What was your plan, Fiona? Why throw them at me now?'

Understanding his anger, she almost retreated behind apologies, but her pride couldn't let him accuse her of shallow cruelty.

'Do you *really* think I'm enjoying this, Byrne? Do you think it was fun for me to keep this to myself for three long years?'

His jaw tightened. 'Why did you come to the ball? Why bother with the pretence of being neighbourly?'

'I—I was trying to find the right time to talk to you. I knew you were grieving, and I knew this was going to be a terrible blow. I thought if I got to know you first it might help.'

'So it's all been an act to get under my guard.' His

lip curled cruelly. 'You have a strange idea of how to help someone.'

'Byrne,' she said quietly, in a desperate bid to sound both sympathetic and reasonable. 'I understand that you hate me for this. It's a hateful situation. But I felt I had to think of Riley. If she's my niece—'

'Your niece?' he shouted. And then, as her meaning sank in, he groaned and closed his eyes.

'I had to consider the possibility that Riley might be entitled to a share of my brother's estate. There was provision for it in his will.'

His eyes snapped open. Grey sparks of blistering anger. 'She doesn't need McLaren's money.' His right hand formed a pistol and he pointed it at her. 'Riley is my daughter. I was there with her mother when she was born and I've been her father from the moment she drew breath. I don't care what you think you can prove. You're not getting near her. Do you hear? I'm her father, and I can provide for her.'

Fiona opened her mouth to reply, but Byrne had already executed a swift about turn and was hurrying out of the house. Seconds later, she heard the slam of his car door and then the motor rev.

She'd failed.

In a miserable daze, Fiona wandered back into her kitchen, her chest a cavern of fire. She set the kettle to boil again, and made a mug of peppermint tea to try to ease the churning in her stomach.

And as she sipped the tea she tried, desperately, to find something positive to cling to. Perhaps she shouldn't be too hard on herself. She hadn't failed, exactly. She'd half expected Byrne's reaction, had known she wouldn't be able to jump from, *'By the way Byrne, I don't think your daughter is your daughter,'* straight into *'Where do you want to take it from here?'*

But she hadn't expected to feel so very bad about it.

CHAPTER SIX

EVERY head in the doctor's waiting room turned when Byrne walked in. Mothers, small children and elderly folk all stared at him with mild surprise, as if they clearly felt that a tall, strapping young cattleman, bursting with vitality and health, should not be taking up their good doctor's precious time.

However, Dr Michael Henderson, Gundawarra's sole GP, was more convivial when his friend strode into his surgery.

'Byrne, good to see you. Take a seat.' He greeted him with just the right balance of friendly warmth and professional distance.

Byrne sat very straight and Michael sat back, relaxed, elbows resting on the arms of his leather chair, and smiled. 'What can I do for you?'

It was the moment Byrne had been dreading ever since he'd left White Cliffs. The permanent bunch of knots in the pit of his stomach tightened. 'I—' He cleared his throat and tried again. 'I think I'm going to need a DNA test.'

'You *think* you'll need one?' Michael repeated calmly but carefully.

Byrne shifted uncomfortably, felt a trickle of sweat run from under his collar and down his spine. 'DNA testing is the best way to prove paternity, isn't it?'

Michael nodded. 'It is.' He sat forward and picked up a pen from his desk. 'We can take mouth swabs here and send them away for testing.' He shot Byrne a cautious glance. 'If you want an indisputable DNA test, we'll need swab samples from you and the child.'

Michael dipped his head and eyed Byrne over the tops of his half-spectacles. 'Is Riley the child in question?'

'Well, of course, man.' Byrne stared at his friend in angry disbelief. 'Who else would it be? Do you think I've been sowing wild oats? Playing the merry widower?'

'I just wanted to be certain, Byrne.'

And I'm overreacting.

Byrne took a deep breath in an effort to calm the fear crawling through him.

Michael cleared his throat. 'A DNA test might not be necessary, actually.'

'Why not?'

'Sometimes, if there are blood incompatibilities...'

Byrne frowned. His eyes narrowed, and a new prickle of alarm snaked over his skin. 'What are you talking about?'

Michael swivelled his chair so that he could check his computer. 'You're a regular blood donor, so we have your group recorded here.'

'Yes, I know. I'm O-positive.'

'Mmm.' Michael, watching the screen, clicked the

mouse, and a second later the hum of the printer began. 'And we have Riley's blood group, too. It was sent to us after the accident, along with other records from the Townsville Hospital.'

There was a brief pause while he scrolled through pages on the screen and found the relevant document. 'I'll print hers for you, too.'

'Wait,' Byrne's heart had begun to thump wildly. 'What can a blood group show? I'm no scientist, but I know there aren't many different blood types. Millions of people can be in the same group.'

'You're right. But blood types can be helpful if there's a clear case of incompatibility between a possible father and a child.'

Byrne's heart beat so hard, it rammed into his throat. He didn't need a clairvoyant to tell him that Michael was about to confirm what the photographs had suggested.

Unbearably tense, he willed himself to stay still as Michael, with painstaking care, set the two sheets of paper on the desk in front of him and used his pen as a pointer. 'Here is your blood group, which is O-positive, as you know. And here is Riley's.'

'She's AB.'

'Yes.'

'And what you're not telling me is that O-positive and AB cannot be a match. They're incompatible, aren't they?'

Michael's face lost its professional mask, and his dark eyes shimmered with compassion. 'I'm afraid so, Byrne.' He spoke with infinite gentleness. 'It isn't possible for a man whose blood group is O to father a child with AB blood.'

So there it was.

Scamp—not his.

Oh, God.

He was falling, like a tree branch snapped off in a howling storm, falling into a bottomless, airless void. He couldn't breathe. Couldn't think, couldn't shift his mind past one horrifying, appalling fact.

Riley, his Scamp, wasn't his at all.

He'd been trying to get his head around this possibility ever since Fiona had showed him the photos, but he'd clung to a hope, a thin, fragile, desperate hope, that the photos had been misleading.

He'd loved Riley from the moment Tessa had discovered she was pregnant straight after their honeymoon. He'd loved her as he'd watched Tessa's waistline expand, as he'd felt the first tiny, fluttering kicks growing stronger week by week. He'd completely lost his heart the instant he'd seen that tiny little body slip into this world, had seen her scrunched red face.

The image of her in that moment, clenched fists, trembling lower lip, her little mouth opening to emit her first bleating cry, were imprinted on him for all time.

His daughter. Their daughter. His and Tessa's.

But now.

Now there was no doubt. The child who'd been christened Riley Therese Drummond was not and never had been his daughter.

'Byrne, I know this must be a terrible blow.'

Byrne stared sightlessly at the floor, his mind eddying and swirling like a log tossed by muddy flood waters.

'You don't look too good, Byrne. How do you feel?'

He blinked and looked up. 'How do I feel? What do you think?' He cracked an angry, sarcastic smile. 'I'm absolutely peachy, doc. Calm as a bloody millpond.'

Michael waited a beat or two, and then said, 'This doesn't have to change anything. You know that, don't you? You're still Riley's father just as you've always been.'

Byrne saw the intent way Michael was watching him, and something clicked in his brain. 'You knew, didn't you?' He leapt to his feet. 'You've known all along.'

Michael looked away.

Hands shaking, Byrne snatched the papers from the desk and shoved them under the doctor's nose. 'How could you keep something like this to yourself?' He stared at his friend. 'How long? How long have you known?' When there was no answer he prompted, 'Ever since she was born?'

'No. No, Byrne.'

'Since the accident, then?'

Michael sighed. And then he nodded.

Byrne's jaw sagged. He couldn't believe this. First Fiona McLaren had hoarded her sordid secret about his personal business, and now one of his best friends had done the same thing.

For three years they'd both known.

'Why the hell didn't you tell me?'

Michael stood abruptly, gripped Byrne's arm. 'Steady on, Byrne. I'm your doctor. And I'm Riley's doctor, too. I'll discuss any aspect of her health with you, but the issue of paternity is not really a medical matter. It isn't strictly my business.'

Jerking his elbow free, Byrne stared at him in disbelief. 'How bloody convenient to hide behind medical ethics. What about our friendship? Doesn't that mean anything? Doesn't it make a difference?'

'You'd just lost your wife, Byrne. It was such a bad time for you. You were deeply grieving. You *needed* your daughter.'

Remembering, Byrne sighed heavily.

'Sit down.' Michael patted Byrne's shoulder. 'You need a moment to get over the shock.'

Byrne sat, closed his eyes and let his head rest back against the wall behind him. He knew Michael's explanation made crazy but justifiable sense. It was almost exactly the same reason Fiona had remained silent. Damn.

Suddenly, he remembered the roomful of patients waiting outside. 'I shouldn't take up any more of your time.'

Both men stood again, and Michael threw an arm around Byrne's shoulders. 'You mustn't let this change anything, Byrne. Riley is your daughter in every way, has been since the moment I delivered her.'

Byrne slanted him a wan smile. 'I'm all the poor kid's got.'

'Don't forget your friends. We're still here for you, mate.'

'Thanks,' Byrne said, shaking his hand.

It wasn't until he'd left the surgery and had stepped out into the dry wall of noonday heat that he remembered—he wasn't the sum total of Riley's family. She had someone else, a flesh-and-blood relative. Her aunt, Fiona McLaren.

And that was another very good reason for keeping the McLaren woman at bay.

* * *

Over the next fortnight, the Gundawarra district was hit by a prolonged heatwave. Relentlessly, day after day, White Cliffs sweltered with temperatures above thirty-five degrees Celsius, and the nights didn't bring much relief.

Fiona slept naked beneath a ceiling fan, with only a light cotton sheet to cover her and with all the windows open in a vain attempt to catch the tiniest breeze.

Then the house was invaded by moths and beetles, attracted by the light of her reading lamp. She found mosquito nets in a cupboard and tried to hang one of them over her bed, but it smelled musty and felt claustrophobic, so she abandoned it, gave up trying to read in bed, and kept a mosquito coil burning.

Then she had trouble sleeping, worried that a spark might fly onto the furniture or onto the spotted gum floorboards. Visions of burning the whole wooden homestead down haunted her.

She was successful, however, in hiring a builder, and the renovations and improvements commenced, beginning with a brand new bathroom.

Every day, as she thumbed through decorating books and rang around the country, searching for exactly the right kind of kitchen cupboards, or the perfect light fittings, thoughts of Byrne Drummond ambushed her. And every night as she lay in bed, amidst the smell of sawdust and new paint, she thought of him, worried about him, dreamed of him and longed to know how he was faring.

Eventually, she could bear it no longer. One midweek evening around eight, when she knew there was a good chance Byrne would be home, she rang Coolaroo's number. And then she stood, clutching the phone, while butterflies danced in her stomach, beating frantic wings against her insides.

Until she heard his deep voice.

'Coolaroo Station.'

'Byrne.' She swallowed. 'It's Fiona McLaren here.'

'Good evening, Fiona.' His response was cool. No 'How are you?' or 'How can I help you?'

'I wanted to make contact. You mentioned something, some time back, about a problem on White Cliffs. With fire breaks. And my fences. Cattle getting through.'

'Yes.'

'I was hoping you could offer some advice about how I should address them.'

In the silence that followed, Fiona closed her eyes and willed herself to stay calm.

At last Byrne said, 'You should be able to find someone with a dozer and a slasher to push fire breaks for you.'

'A dozer and a slasher,' Fiona repeated, writing this down.

'Check out young Ben Phillips. He's in the phone book. And there are plenty of fencing contractors available at this time of year. The stock and station agency in town will give you a list.'

'All right. Thanks.'

'That's all you wanted?' he asked coolly.

No. She had a thousand questions.

She wanted to know how Byrne was feeling, *really* feeling, whether he was adjusting OK, whether he and Riley were still close. She couldn't bear to think that their father-daughter relationship had been harmed.

And, although she knew it was asking too much, she

longed to be invited to meet her niece properly, to have the chance to get to know her.

She fiddled with the phone cord. 'How are you, Byrne? Are you—OK?'

'Of course. I'm fine. Anything else?'

So clipped. So final. So clearly hiding the truth. But the warning was clear: *Stay out of my life.*

No point in prolonging this call.

Suppressing a sigh, she admitted defeat. 'No, that was all I was after, Byrne. Thanks for your help.'

'You're welcome. Good night.'

She set the receiver down and went through to the kitchen to look for antacid to ease the pain in her stomach.

How silly of her to care so deeply about a man who was not and never would be interested in her in any way.

As the third week of the heatwave dawned, dark thunder clouds rolled in from the north and brooded and hovered over Gundawarra. All through the long, simmering day, the clouds pressed low, purple as bruises. The air was oppressively humid and heavy, draining everyone's energy. Mid-afternoon, thunder rumbled, but didn't bring the longed-for rain. At teatime Riley was fretful, and declared she wasn't hungry.

As Byrne tried to settle her to sleep, a fierce crack of lightning exploded close by, so close that he wondered if one of Coolaroo's trees had been struck.

Riley clutched his hand. 'Daddy, don't leave me. I'm scared.'

'I'll stay, Scamp, but don't be frightened.' In the darkness, he stroked her hair. 'It's only noise, it can't hurt you. Just like fireworks, lots of loud noise and bright lights.'

'It hurts my ears. It's too loud, Daddy. I don't like it.'

'Ssh... Don't worry. Lightning is good.'

She turned her head, her eyes narrowed with disbelief. 'How is it good?'

'It puts nitrogen back into the soil, and it helps grass to grow sweet so the cattle get fat.'

'Oh,' she said, suitably impressed.

'If we're lucky we'll get some really good rain out of this storm.'

'I like rain.'

'Yes. Now snuggle down.'

She snuggled obediently, hugging her threadbare treasures, Dunkum and Athengar. Closing her eyes, she curled into a little ball, and Byrne tucked a pink cotton-weave blanket around her and sat on the edge of her bed, stroking her silky, straight hair.

In the faint moonlight he saw the dark curve of her eyelashes lying against her plump cheek like thick little commas, and he felt a familiar, warm glow of fatherly love wash over and through him. She really was the cutest little thing.

But he couldn't think fondly about her without letting in other feelings. Ever since he'd left Mike Henderson's surgery, a mix of anger and deprivation had rolled around inside him. It hurt to know that his genes, his blood, had not been inherited by this beautiful little human being.

But, hell, he was determined not to let that interfere with the strong emotional bonds he had with the kid.

Those feelings had always been there, even before Tessa had died, but more strongly since.

Scamp was all he had. He'd missed his chance for more children. He had no brothers and the Drummond line was coming to an end.

He sat very still, fighting an urge to give in to despair, and heard the first fat drops of rain hitting the ground outside the bedroom window. In the distance, there was another low growl of thunder.

Eventually, he heard Riley's regular, soft breathing, and he dropped a light kiss on her cheek and tiptoed out of the room and onto the verandah, where he looked out into the night. So far, there'd been very little rain with the storm, and it seemed that already it was over. He wondered again about the lightning that had struck close by, but couldn't see any sign of a tree on fire.

On the verandah, he sat in the dark in an old squatter's chair, as he had every evening for weeks now. Before that he'd always spent his evenings reading, or lounging in front of the television. Sometimes he'd worked on accounting matters in his study. But these days his mind was too troubled to settle to any of these activities. He'd become as brooding and remote as he'd been three years ago, after the accident.

He hadn't even gone to Jane and Mitch Layton's monthly pot-luck dinner. Three sets of friends had rung the next day to check that he was OK, and he'd been brusque with all of them.

Now he stared into the night and wished, as he had

so many times, that Fiona McLaren had stayed in Sydney and kept her black family secrets to herself.

And then, as he looked through the dark bush in the direction of White Cliffs, he found his thoughts creeping, like mutinous pirates, in the very direction he wanted to avoid. With an unwilling, twisted smile, he wondered if Fiona was frightened by thunder and lightning.

He could picture her alone in bed, her hair like flames against her pillow. He remembered their kiss at the ball, an incident he'd recalled far too many times. And his body reacted the way it always did, as if she was already there in his arms. He could taste her mouth, lush and sweet, feel her body, pliant and womanly, pressing into him.

With an angry mutter, he jumped to his feet and strode to the far end of the verandah. It angered him that his body could want Fiona, while her blood ties with his daughter left him bitter and hollow with resentment.

Worse was the nagging, crazy idea that she had more going for her than mere sex appeal. He couldn't deny a grudging admiration for her brains and gutsy attitude.

Under other circumstances, he might have sought her company.

Pull your head in, man. These circumstances are here to stay.

And he would never be at peace until he deleted Ms McLaren and her family from his thoughts.

CHAPTER SEVEN

FIONA woke in a panic, and jack-knifed into a sitting position before she was properly conscious. Her heart pounded as she listened to the night, trying to recognize the sound that had woken her. Had it been part of her dreams or real?

The thunder and lightning had finished hours ago, but now there was a wild wind howling outside. Was that what had woken her?

Hadn't there been something else?

And then she heard it, the sound that had invaded her sleep and laid a clammy hand on her heart, chilling her bones.

Crackling. Snapping. And spitting.

A kind of roaring swoosh.

And a smell, the acrid smell of—

Heavens, no!

Heart in mouth, she flung her sheet aside, dashed to the bedroom window and ripped the curtains apart. The entire hillside was on fire.

Panic exploded through her. The fire was huge. It

covered most of the horizon behind the homestead, a massive, burning ridge standing out starkly against the inky black of the night sky. A wall of bright red flames was racing down the slope towards the house.

What could she do? She was alone. A helpless city girl with absolutely no experience of bush fires.

You'll die if you panic. Think or you'll sink.

A huge blast of hot air hit her, and the wind shook the house, jolting her into action. Shaking, she raced to the telephone and dialled 000.

'I need the Gundawarra fire brigade,' she shouted, and felt sick to hear how scared she sounded. But calmness was beyond her. The roar of the fire was getting louder every minute. 'I'm on a cattle property. White Cliffs, about fifteen kilometres out of town on the road to Tilba. There's a bush fire here. It's huge, and it's heading for my house.'

A calm voice on the other end told her they'd already received a call. 'The fire brigade is on its way.'

'Oh, great. What should I do? Should I try to get out of here?'

'It would be too much of a risk. Best to wait at the house. They shouldn't be too long.'

'How long?'

'Oh...' After a pause, 'About twenty minutes.'

Twenty minutes. She could be cinders by then.

She raced to the window again. Already, the fire was closer. A big fireball was rolling across the massive, leafy tops of giant gum trees, powering directly towards her, leaving a trail of fiery red and gold crowns in its wake. Fire from below joined the fire above, and the trees exploded, one after the other. Rivers of bright flame snaked down the hillside at an alarming speed.

Fiona wished she hadn't been instructed to stay with the house. Surely she would be better to try to make a dash in her car for the river? She thought of Byrne Drummond. He'd lived here all his life; he'd know what to do. She decided to ring him. After all, he was her nearest neighbour and this was a dire emergency.

At that very moment, the telephone rang, and it was so unexpected she jumped, but then she darted across the room and snatched it up on the second ring.

'Hello.'

'Fiona, Byrne here.'

'Oh, thank heavens, Byrne. I was about to ring you.'

'Are you OK?'

'No, not really. There's a bush fire here. Have you seen it? It's coming straight for my house.'

'Yeah. I saw it from my place. I'm on my way over.'

'Oh, Byrne, that's wonderful. Thank you.' Above the roar of the fire, she shouted, 'Can you hurry? I'm kind of panicking. I haven't got a clue what to do.'

'I'm coming as fast as I can, but it could take me ten minutes.'

'Ten?' There was no way she could keep the panic from her voice.

'I've rung the fire brigade,' he said. 'They're on their way too.'

'I know, but they're going to take ages. Byrne, what should I do? I've been told to stay at the house, but don't you think I should try to get down to the river?'

'How far from the house is the fire?'

'Hang on, I'll have another look.'

She dashed to the window, then back. 'It's only about two hundred metres away.'

'You'll have to stay in the house, then. You'll never make it to the river. Late evacuation is too dangerous.'

'Oh, God.'

'Now don't worry, Fiona. You're better off inside the house.'

She wished she could feel more confident about that. 'Maybe I should get in my car? I could drive down to the road.'

'Too risky,' he said. 'From what I can tell, the fire front seems to be sweeping along the White Cliffs road already.'

'Then how will you get here?'

'I'm coming the back way. Across country.'

'I could do that, too, couldn't I?'

'You don't know the way, and it's a dark night. You'll probably hit a tree stump or run into a gully. Wait for me. I promise I'll be there soon. Just do what I tell you and you'll be OK.'

She gulped. 'All right. Tell me what to do, then. Please.'

'First, keep in touch. The overhead wires could burn and then we'd lose contact, so ring me back on your mobile.'

'Oh, good thinking. Hang on. It's in the next room.'

She was back in a matter of seconds, punching digits as Byrne dictated his number. Then, with a tiny pang of fear, she hung up the house phone, dialled on her mobile and almost wept with joy when Byrne answered.

'What now?' she asked, panting a little.

'You need to be well protected. What are you wearing?'

'Um.' She glanced down. 'Nothing, actually.'

There was a choked exclamation which might have been a curse. It was hard to hear over the roaring and crackling outside.

'You need protection from the radiant heat,' he said. 'Hurry and put on strong clothes that will cover you well. Jeans, a long-sleeved woollen sweater, sturdy shoes, leather boots if you've got them, and a hat, too.'

'OK.'

'And shut every window and door so sparks can't fly in.'

With a quick word of thanks, Fiona fled, grateful for Byrne's instructions. Practical tasks helped keep the panic at bay.

As she dragged on jeans, a sweater and boots the air about her grew hotter and the roar of the fire more thunderous. And as she ran through the house, slamming windows shut, she caught frightening glimpses of burning tree branches flying through the air. The terrifying wall of angry orange and red flames leapt up into the black night, eating up grass and trees as it charged towards her.

'Are you there, Byrne?'

'Yes. How are you?'

'Not very happy. The fire's getting closer.'

And then all the lights went out. Fiona yelped in alarm.

'Are you there? What happened?'

'I've just lost power. Oh, God, I'm so scared, Byrne. Where are you?'

'Not far away now.'

'I need you here.' Her voice broke on a sob.

'You're going to be OK. You're a smart, brave girl. You're going to be fine.'

He spoke in such a warm, certain tone that she willed herself to believe him.

'But it's going to get very hot in there,' he said. 'You need to keep yourself well protected. Grab plenty of blankets to throw over you.'

The glow of the approaching fire sent a ghastly red light through the darkened house as she headed for a linen press in the hall. 'Got the blankets.'

'And a water bottle, too. Drink plenty of water, so you don't dehydrate.'

'OK, I'm off to the kitchen now.'

'Good girl.'

'Byrne?'

'Yes.'

Gripping her cell phone between her jaw and her shoulder as she snagged a water bottle from the fridge, she said, 'Thanks so much for this.'

The kitchen was at the opposite end of the house from the fire, and Fiona decided that she would stay there, close to the solid metal coolness of the refrigerator. But she couldn't stay still. In no time at all her anxiety took hold again, and she hurried to the window.

A car horn sounded and then, to the south, she saw twin yellow lights bobbing through the blackness.

Byrne. Thank heavens.

Clutching her blankets, phone and water bottle, she watched his vehicle draw closer and then, as he reached the lawn, she burst through the doorway, almost flung herself down the front steps and stumbled across the grass.

Byrne's Land Cruiser screeched to a halt and he was beside her in an instant, his arms about her, hauling her close. She had never felt so swamped with relief. He felt so strong, like a mountain. But, too soon, he gently set her aside and reached back into his vehicle to retrieve a large torch. 'Wait here while I check things out.'

Fiona waited, clutching the blankets, while Byrne did a quick circuit of the homestead. She watched him turn on a tap, heard his curse when only a thin trickle emerged.

'That bloody manager of yours was as lazy as it gets,' he shouted above the roar of the rapidly advancing front. 'We won't be able to defend the house.'

'Not enough water pressure?' she asked as he hurried back to her.

'Not only that. The fire break around the back is all overgrown. There's nothing to stop a blaze from burning right up to the building. Nothing we do in the next few minutes will help.'

'What about the fire brigade?'

'They might be too late.' Byrne stared grimly at the house and shook his head. 'Normally a building would be the safest place.' He stopped and muttered something Fiona couldn't hear.

'What'll we do, then?'

'Get out of here. Pronto.' He grabbed her elbow.

'But you said—'

She cast a despairing glance back to the house. It looked so vulnerable. Helpless. She hadn't lived there for long, but the house had so much potential. The bathroom was lovely now, and she hated the thought of abandoning it to the fire.

'My renovations,' she cried, feeling foolish but sad.

'C'mon. There's no time, Fiona.'

The wind showered a spray of sparks onto the homestead roof, and Byrne wrenched the car's passenger door open and shoved her towards it. 'Get in. I don't intend to spend my last few minutes on this earth arguing with a stubborn redhead.'

Chastened, she quickly scrambled into the car, and almost immediately Byrne was in his seat beside her. His door slammed shut and he turned to her.

His eyes shone through the darkness with a brilliance that caught her by surprise. He was looking at her with such unexpected tenderness that she forgave him for manhandling her.

'Fasten your seatbelt,' he said, and his gaze snapped to the front and the big white four-wheel-drive took off, bouncing across the home paddock.

He flicked a switch on the dashboard and a set of huge spotlights lit up their path for hundreds of metres, sending a faint, silvery backwash through the truck's cabin, and Fiona couldn't resist stealing glimpses of Byrne's profile while he concentrated on his task.

He was so ruggedly handsome, his face a perfect mix of masculine planes and angles. But it was hardly a time for indulging her fantasies, so she looked ahead again.

'Byrne, watch out. There's a fence.'

He didn't answer and, to her amazement, he drove straight through the strands of barbed wire, the wires bursting before them with a sharp, metallic twang.

Then she looked back and saw the homestead framed by a massive wall of orange and red flames. It was horrendous, like a scene from a horror movie, and it was almost impossible to accept that it was really happening. Twenty minutes ago she'd been sound asleep in there.

Tears burned her eyes and she leaned a little closer to Byrne, seeking comfort, but the vehicle bounced over a very rough patch of ground and she was rudely jolted back against the door. Next minute, they dived straight into a big stand of ironbark and wattle trees.

With a skilful gear-shift change, Byrne wove past the big tree trunks and smashed through low undergrowth. Branches whipped past the windscreen, scratched against the side of the vehicle.

As they topped a small ridge and made their way downhill, Fiona turned back for another glimpse of the house. She couldn't find it, and twisted harder, searching through the rear window, but there were flames everywhere.

'What do you think is happening back there?'

'We can't afford to hang around to find out.'

The vehicle suddenly pitched forward, and there were more furious gear changes as they dropped headlong down an almost vertical bank into a deeply eroded creek bed. For a terrifying moment, the wheels sank and spun in the loose sand.

'We're stuck, aren't we?' Fiona whispered, fighting terrifying visions of them trapped in the path of the fire.

Byrne flashed her a quick grin. 'I'll hand in my driver's licence if I can't get this old girl out of here.'

Pushing another lever, he sent the motor into a low growl, and the vehicle seemed to almost waddle across the sand, as if the wheels had become webbed feet. And then it climbed rapidly up the steep incline of the bank.

'With a little luck that creek bed will buy us some time and distance as a temporary firebreak,' he said, and once more they were bouncing through light scrub, dodging logs and boulders.

He nodded in the direction of the fire, which was still setting the night sky aglow, but looked less sinister from this distance.

'We've put some distance between us and the front. But I'm going to cut across to the east now to get right away from it. If the wind really comes up with a decent blow, we don't want to be in front of it. A big fire like that with some breeze behind it can move faster than we can drive across rough country.'

Fiona shuddered. 'I would have died without you.'

'You were very brave,' he said.

'I was a mess.'

He grinned. 'But you weren't hysterical.'

'Only because I knew you were coming.'

The vehicle slowed, then came to a halt with the motor still running. Through the shadows, Byrne looked at her and then, to her surprise, he unsnapped her seatbelt and drew her against his shoulder. She felt the rough cotton of his work shirt beneath her cheek, and the warm pressure of his jaw caressing her forehead.

She knew his kindness was simply the response of one neighbour helping another in a time of dire emergency, but just the same, when he held her close, every cell in her body responded. She could smell his skin, see the dark shadow of his throat inches from her, and she longed to bury her face into the curve of his neck, to absorb his strength, absorb him.

A siren sounded, and he turned away and looked out into the night.

'There goes the fire tender from Gundawarra.'

Lifting her head, she saw headlights off to their right, flickering through the black trees towards the ghastly red glow.

'Should we let them know we're safe?'

'Sure.' He reached for his phone. 'I'll ring through to tell them I've got you with me.'

Once he dealt with that, he said, 'There's nothing we can do to help at White Cliffs now. I'd better take you home.'

Home.

She was silenced by the very thought of going to Byrne's house. Despite everything, the horror of the fire and of watching it threaten her house, she couldn't help feeling just a little uplifted by the thought of entering Byrne Drummond's private domain.

They drove on, rattling over the low wooden bridge that crossed the river, and then along a rough bush track, and Fiona relaxed back into her seat and stared out into the night. Slim tree-trunks rushed past, their bark turning briefly to silver in the flash of the passing headlights. She yawned and realised how tired she was, felt a little chilled and drew one of the blankets around her.

Her eyes drifted shut, and she might have nodded off if Byrne hadn't spoken.

'Won't be long now.'

Opening her eyes again, she saw that they were

turning at the end of a fence line onto a smoother, wider track.

Peering ahead, she caught a shimmer of silver, and guessed it was the iron roof of Coolaroo homestead. She yawned again and asked sleepily, 'Do you know what time it is?'

'About two a.m.' Byrne flashed her a quick grin. 'You'll be able to tumble straight into bed. Our spare room is always made up and ready for visitors.'

He dimmed the headlights as they approached the house, but she could see a curving line of tall Bunya pine trees, and beyond them a smooth sweep of lawn, and a long, low, timber homestead painted white. A light appeared on the verandah, spilling yellow onto the lawn, and she saw neat sections of white lattice, huge hanging baskets overflowing with lush ferns, pots of bright purple bougainvillea.

As soon as the vehicle stopped, Byrne was out and opening her door for her. 'If I know Ellen, she'll have the kettle on already,' he said.

'Ellen?'

'Ellen Jackson. My housekeeper.'

Of course. Fiona hadn't given much thought to Byrne's domestic arrangements, but now she found herself hoping, rather ungraciously, that Ellen Jackson wasn't young and pretty.

The front door opened, and they were greeted by a grey haired, cheery faced woman, round and motherly in her pink quilted dressing gown and blue fluffy slippers.

'There you are.' It was clearly Ellen, and she beamed

at Fiona. 'I'm so glad you're safe, love.' She turned to Byrne. 'Was it bad?'

'Bad enough. I don't know if the fire brigade will be able to save the homestead.'

'Dear, oh, dear.' Ellen's expressive face was an instant picture of sympathy, and she held out her arms and enveloped Fiona in a bear hug. 'You poor lamb. Come on in. At least we can offer you a bed and a nice cup of hot tea.'

She led the way down a central hallway to a big kitchen at the back of the house, and as Fiona followed she was delighted by the comfortable ambience of Byrne's home.

Gleaming timber floors were carpeted with Persian rugs in rich hues of claret, royal blue and cream. Elegant lamps cast a warm glow. A cosy corner with a deep armchair nestled beside tall shelves of books, and a mirror-backed, silky oak sideboard sported a huge glass jug overflowing with scarlet banksia blossoms and creamy wild orchids.

And the kitchen, large, casual and unfashionably cluttered, was wonderfully inviting with honey toned timber floors and blue gingham curtains. Chairs painted red were gathered around a big pine table.

It was exactly the kind of kitchen Fiona had been aiming for at White Cliffs. She saw a picture of that house as she'd last seen it, about to be engulfed in flames, and tears sprang to her eyes.

'Here, love, sit down.' Ellen pulled out one of the red chairs. 'You've had a terrible ordeal and you're worn out.'

'Thanks.'

Ellen set a steaming mug of tea in front of Fiona and a plate of home-made shortbread.

'Get a little something in your stomach and then hop straight into bed.' She was kindness personified, the kind of motherly figure who had never featured in Fiona's life.

Sipping hot, sweet tea, Fiona looked about her, wondered where Byrne had got to, and then heard his booted footsteps in the hall.

'I've been talking to the fire brigade,' he said. 'They've got most of the blaze under control.'

'Already? That's good. What about the house?'

He shook his head. 'I'm afraid they couldn't save much.'

She nodded, and waited to be overwhelmed by sadness. Instead, she felt suddenly calm, and was a little disconcerted to realise it was because Byrne was there, watching her with a gentle light in his eyes and no hint of his former hostility.

CHAPTER EIGHT

FIONA was late for breakfast next morning. Byrne had been up since six and he, Scamp, Ellen and her husband, Ted, were already halfway through breakfast.

Fiona wandered in, still dressed in the same khaki shirt and blue jeans she'd dragged on last night, looking pale and tired and vulnerable, with mauve shadows beneath her eyes, her auburn hair sleep-tumbled.

Damn, Byrne thought, and his stomach tightened. Fiona was one of those rare women who looked dangerously sexy first thing in the morning.

'I thought I heard voices,' she said. 'What time is it?'

'Almost time for me to go to school,' Riley announced self-importantly. She was dressed and ready in her school uniform, and she looked up at Fiona with huge, curious eyes. 'Did your house really burn down?'

Byrne quickly intervened. 'Let Fiona sit down before you bombard her with questions.'

Riley turned to him instead. 'Will our house burn down too, Daddy?'

'No,' he said, and he gave her nose a playful tweak. 'Why not?'

'Because your daddy looks after Coolaroo,' Fiona said, before anybody else could answer. 'He keeps good fire breaks.'

Across the table, her green eyes met Byrne's and a corner of her mouth lifted just a little, making her look sexier than ever. Byrne swallowed a piece of toast and it stuck in his throat.

Ellen was on her feet and halfway to the stove where a pan sizzled with eggs and bacon. 'You'll have a full breakfast, won't you, Fiona?'

'Oh, just some tea and toast will be fine, thanks.'

Riley eyed her mischievously. 'Why don't you have bacon and eggs? They put hairs on your chest.'

'Hairs on my chest?'

'Scamp!' Byrne struggled to ignore a sudden vision of Fiona's chest—naked, pale, her breasts white and generously round, pink-tipped. 'That's no way to speak to a lady.'

'But that's what Ted tells me,' Scamp protested. 'Don't you, Ted?'

The kitchen was suddenly awash with discomfort. Riley looked upset. Ellen sent her husband a baleful glare, thumped her hands on her hips and rolled her eyes to the ceiling. Ted looked sheepish. A flush bloomed in Fiona's cheeks.

'Isn't it time you got ready for the school bus?' Byrne said.

Everyone seemed to welcome the diversion. Ellen began to fuss about Riley's lunch box. Ted went to fetch the ute, and by the time Riley had left with him to meet the school bus that called past Coolaroo's front gate

Fiona had finished one cup of tea, had poured another and was spreading a second slice of toast with Ellen's excellent marmalade.

'I'm going to ride over to White Cliffs to check out the damage,' Byrne told her. 'I thought I might bring some of the White Cliffs cattle back onto Coolaroo for the time being. I can keep them here until the fences are repaired.'

Fiona set down her knife. 'I'd like to come with you. To help.'

He frowned. 'Shouldn't you be taking it easy today?'

'I feel fine, Byrne.'

This was a complication he hadn't bargained for. 'I was planning to go by horse. I'll be looking for frightened cattle tucked away in all sorts of hard-to-find places.'

'I'd still like to come.'

'Can you ride?'

'Yes.' Her chin lifted and her green eyes flashed, defying him to challenge her.

The thought of having her with him for a whole day flustered him, sent thrusts of masculine hunger driving low. He searched for a way out. 'Aren't you frightened of horses?'

'Only when I'm on the ground beside a huge stallion that's prancing about. I'll be OK once I'm up in the saddle, especially if you've got a quieter horse.'

She watched him, her eyes wide and eager, waiting for his answer. Then, quite unexpectedly, her perky confidence took a dive and she gave an embarrassed shrug. Had he scowled at her? More than likely.

'All right,' she said. 'I'll admit, it's been a while since I've ridden a horse.'

'How long?'

She mumbled a figure.

'*How* long?'

'A few years. Five or six. But when I was at school I spent all my summer holidays on my uncle's farm. Later, I escaped for horse-riding weekends whenever I could afford them. Then I got too busy at work, but I'm sure it will come back to me.'

There was a stubborn determination about this woman that reminded Byrne of Riley.

And, of course, there was a very obvious reason for that. A pang of dismay burned deep, making him flinch.

'I'd really like to come, Byrne,' she said gently.

'It'll be a long day. You'll be stiff and sore.'

She sighed and looked down at her toast, picked up her knife and cut the toast in half. 'I suppose that's a polite way of saying I'll be too big a handicap.'

Here was his chance. To be free of Fiona McLaren. A whole day without her. Wasn't that what he wanted?

He pictured her in the saddle, riding beside him, slanting him green-eyed smiles from beneath a shady hat, thought of the long, lonely years he'd ridden alone and how he'd always tried not to mind that Tessa had shown little interest in Coolaroo beyond the homestead. He drew a sharp breath.

'I'll find you a quiet horse and you can have a trial run in the home paddock.'

There was a scary moment when Fiona didn't think she could get on the horse. The mare, called Grey Lady, waited patiently enough. But the saddle seemed to be

such a long way from the ground, further than she remembered, and she'd stretched the truth when she'd
told Byrne it was five or six years since she'd been on
a horse. It was closer to ten.

But she knew she mustn't show any sign of fear.
Byrne would grab the first excuse to leave her behind,
so she took the reins, set her foot in the stirrup and
swung her leg up and over the big, high back.

To her relief, Grey Lady didn't flinch, didn't move.
Fiona took a deep breath, let it out and took another.
Setting her shoulders back, she sat straight in the saddle,
held the reins lightly, and sent Byrne a smile from
beneath the shady Akubra he'd lent her.

'All set?' he called.

'Sure am.'

They set off at a walk, and Fiona was nervous under
Byrne's close scrutiny, but Grey Lady was a perfect
darling and Fiona began to relax, to enjoy the feel of the
smooth, worn leather saddle and the rhythm of the horse
beneath her. Once they were through the home paddock
gate, they began to canter, and the joy of being astride
a strong and fluid, sure-footed horse came back with a
cork-from-champagne rush of pleasure.

She knew that all kinds of muscles would be aching
by the end of the day, but she would worry about them
later. For now, she would make the most of a full day in
Byrne's company; she would be a woman of the Outback.

The blackened bush at White Cliffs was still smouldering, so they skirted around it, sobered by the sight of so
much destruction.

Fiona had seen the aftermath of bush fires before, but only from the comfort of her car as she'd zipped along a highway. On those occasions she'd felt a momentary pang for the loss of bush and wildlife. But this loss was personal.

Over the past weeks, she'd developed a deep sense of connection with this land. It hurt now to see the blackened hillside covered in hundreds of lifeless black trunks, to see the bare, blackened earth and rocks where, only a day before, she'd admired silver trunks and branches clothed in soft, blue-green, tapering foliage, knee-high grass the colour of champagne, and the smooth, pale boulders where kangaroos lazed in the sun.

Now, above all the blackness, hawks and crows hovered, and she shuddered to think of the shy bush creatures that had lost their lives.

The clear, beautiful blue sky above all the black looked almost obscene.

Byrne remained stern and silent as he rode beside her, watching her often, with a careful, hooded gaze. 'You'd be surprised how quickly the bush comes back after a fire,' he said. 'In a week or so you'll see a little fringe of green starting to show.'

But then they reached the sickening ruins of the house.

The ripple-iron roof was twisted and sunken, the walls blackened and in some places non-existent. In her bedroom, empty casements hung by their hinges like loose teeth about to fall out.

Byrne turned to her, his eyes dark with sympathy. 'I doubt you'll be able to salvage anything from this.'

She shrugged bravely, sent him a rueful smile. 'Just as well I hadn't got very far with the renovations.'

'You're insured?'

'Yes, the house and contents are covered.'

'What about the stock? Your fences?'

'I'm not sure. I think so.'

She blinked tears as she took a long hard look at the house. Her laptop had been in there, but at least all her important files had been backed up before she'd left Sydney. There were clothes, none of them important, except the dress she'd worn to the Gundawarra ball. Her MP3 player with all her favourite music could be replaced.

But there'd been things of Jamie's. Including the photos.

Those damning photos that had turned Byrne's life upside down were gone now, burnt to cinders.

What cruel irony. Without the evidence in those photos, she might never have come back to White Cliffs, would certainly not have opened up the wound that had hurt Byrne so terribly.

'Seen enough?' he asked her.

She nodded.

'You could probably do with a cup of tea after seeing all this.'

'A cup of tea?' She shot him a puzzled glance.

'We can go down to the river and make billy tea before we start looking for the cattle.'

Billy tea. Of course. She smiled. 'Everything seems better after a cup of tea, doesn't it?'

The fire hadn't burned all the way to the riverbank, and they found a shaded patch of grass overlooking a long, slow bend in the river. Byrne had a billycan and the makings for tea in his saddlebag, and they built a neat fire with brittle twigs, filled the billy with water from the river, and sat and watched the sleepy flow of water as the fire crackled.

It was an idyllic spot, perfect for relaxing, and Fiona tried to ignore the twinges of pain in her lower back, the tightness in her thighs and hips. But she couldn't shrug aside thoughts of Jamie's photos and all the havoc and heartache they'd caused.

'Do you think you'll build a new homestead?' Byrne asked.

She sighed, and her mouth twisted into a wry smile. 'I guess that would depend on who wanted to buy it.'

'I'm still interested.'

She nodded thoughtfully and frowned, cleared her throat. 'In—in my brother's will there was provision for the possibility of offspring. So—so you wouldn't actually have to buy the whole property. Half of it already...' She couldn't quite finish the sentence.

Byrne, sitting with elbows propped on bent knees as he stared into the fire, was silent for so long she wished she hadn't spoken. He'd been so kind to her last night, and again this morning. She'd sensed a fragile bridge building between them. And now, with the mention of Jamie, she'd ruined it.

She chewed her lip as she stared at the seething strings of bubbles forming in the billy.

'Byrne,' she said at last, very gently. 'I'm so disappointed in my brother. I'm truly devastated by what he did. I can't bear knowing that he interfered in your marriage.'

The water came to a rapid boil, bubbling noisily. Byrne tossed a handful of tealeaves into it, used a green twig to stir them, and the water darkened to honey-brown. Selecting a stronger branch as a lever, he lifted the billy from the fire.

He looked at Fiona, his expression carefully controlled, ambiguous, and then switched his gaze back to the embers of the fire. 'If it's any comfort, I don't think my wife committed adultery with your brother.'

Her jaw sagged with surprise.

Byrne set two green enamel mugs on the ground beside the billy, a screw-top jar filled with sugar, and a teaspoon.

'Before we were married, Tessa and I had a rather tempestuous, on-again off-again courtship,' he said without looking at her. 'At one point, we called it all off. Tessa was terribly upset, of course, and she went back to Sydney and took up with an old boyfriend.'

'Jamie?'

Byrne nodded. 'As soon as she'd gone, I realised what a damn fool I'd been. I should have been quicker off the mark, but we had a big cattle muster on the go and I was out in the bush for weeks. First chance I could, I took off after her.' He picked up the billy and poured strong black tea into the two mugs. 'Do you take sugar?'

'If it's black tea, yes, please.'

As he handed her a mug, she said, 'So you went to Sydney and found Tessa? With Jamie?'

'A mutual friend told me she was living in a flat by herself, but she'd been going out with an old boyfriend from university days.'

'What happened when you turned up? Was she pleased to see you?'

He nodded. 'I found her and apologized. Swept her off her feet.' He chanced a small smile. 'We were married within a fortnight.'

Fiona sipped her tea, which was strong and sweet, tasting faintly of smoke, actually pleasantly so, and she thought about Byrne Drummond sweeping a woman off her feet. How thrilling and romantic that must have been. She felt jealousy plunge deep in the pit of her stomach, ridiculous, inappropriate.

'So it's quite possible,' she said carefully, 'that Tessa never knew her baby was Jamie's.'

Byrne looked up from the fire. His smoky grey gaze met hers and didn't waver. 'I'm quite sure Tess never realised.'

Taking another sip of tea, Fiona felt a rush of gladness, of relief. Her brother hadn't violated the Drummonds' marriage. Byrne's wife hadn't deceived her husband.

The world suddenly seemed a better place.

'Thank you for telling me that,' she said.

He drained his mug and lifted the billy. 'Would you like any more?'

'No, this is fine, thanks.'

He poured more tea into his mug, added sugar. A butcher bird landed in the tree above them and broke into a bright, warbling song.

There was one final question Fiona needed to raise. 'Was it merely a coincidence that Jamie bought this property next door to yours?' she asked carefully.

Byrne's jaw tightened. 'It's possible.' Again he looked at her, his grey eyes penetrating hers with a soul-deep intensity that made her heart tremble. 'I guess it's a mystery we'll never solve.'

He tipped the last of his tea onto the smouldering coals, picked up the billy and poured more water onto the embers, then stood and with a booted foot kicked dirt over them until he was satisfied that their fire was completely doused. 'Don't want to start another bush fire.'

Getting back onto Grey Lady was a tad difficult. Fiona was fit from her regular dancing classes, but the muscles used in horse riding were very rarely exercised. By the end of the day, she felt black and blue, more exhausted than she could have thought possible.

When at last she and Byrne rode back to Coolaroo, the blue sky was fading and a twilight moon had risen. The moon was white and full, and framed by a flock of pink and grey galahs perched in the branches of a gum tree. Mobs of quiet kangaroos grazed in purple shadows. Crickets chirped and cicadas hummed.

It was a beautiful time of day in the Outback, but she was too tired and aching to enjoy it, too worried that she would never be able to get out of the saddle.

All day, she'd been determined to keep up with Byrne, to never complain, or to be any trouble. She'd been mega-careful to show no sign of weakness, and she thought she'd been quite amazingly game when she'd helped him to steer an entire mob of frightened cattle out of a rocky gully and up over a ridge into one of Coolaroo's secure paddocks.

When at last they'd closed the gate on the mob he'd smiled and said, 'You've done brilliantly, Fiona.'

And those scant words of praise, and the bright spark of warmth in his eyes, had been enough to fill her from the soles of her feet to her scalp with happiness.

But there'd been times during the day, when Byrne hadn't been looking, that she'd stood in the stirrups, easing her rump from side to side, trying to relieve the strain on her inner thighs and the growing cramp in both hips.

Now she was going to pay for her day in the saddle. Sorely. Her back and shoulders ached, her hips burned and the deep muscles in her rear and lower back were screaming.

Byrne, walking his horse ahead of her, leaned down and released the catch on the gate to the home paddock, waited till she'd passed through and then closed it behind her.

'You can dismount at the steps to the house,' he said. 'I'll look after the horses.'

'What do you have to do for them?'

He shrugged. 'Not much. Wash the sweat off them, give them a feed. Stow the saddles away.'

'Shouldn't I help?'

From beneath his shady Akubra, his grey eyes twinkled. 'No, you shouldn't. You're too tired.'

'Is it that obvious?' She managed a rueful smile.

He chuckled. 'You can hardly keep your eyes open.'

She didn't have the energy to argue, wasn't sure she had the energy to get out of the saddle. In fact she wasn't sure she could move at all.

As she reined Grey Lady to a halt in front of the steps, she was aching all over and, to her horror, she realised that her hips had seized so tightly she couldn't lift her leg.

There was no way she could urge her leg to make that massive journey over the horse's back. She was stuck.

Tears of humiliation stung and she closed her eyes, desperate not to cry.

'Here, let me help you.'

Byrne's deep voice brought her eyes flashing open. She hadn't even noticed him dismount, but now she saw that he'd tethered both their horses to the verandah railing and was standing beside her.

'I'm just a little stiff. After being on a horse all day. I'll be right in a minute.'

'Nothing to be embarrassed about,' he said gently. 'Let's ease your feet out of these stirrups.' She felt his hand firmly grip her booted ankle as he slipped the stirrup free, first on one side then the other. 'Now lean sideways. I'll catch you.'

'No, I can't. You can't.'

'Fiona, don't argue.'

In the end her pain won; she had no choice but to obey him.

Her sideways tumble into his arms was awkward and clumsy, but Byrne caught her easily and held her as if she weighed no more than Riley. She tried one last protest as he carried her up the steps and into the house, but he ignored her, and after that she decided that it was rather wonderful to be cradled by strong, masculine arms.

She couldn't remember ever being carried this way, not even by her father when she was little.

She'd spent so many, many years being strong.

One of the poorest kids in the school yard, she'd

had a tough childhood, and later life had only got tougher. In the corporate world she'd had to stand up to alpha males—lawyers trying to bluff their way through clients' infringements, managing directors scheming to knock a few grand off their bills simply because they thought they could get away with it, because she was a woman.

And now, here was Byrne, carrying her as if she were precious cargo, calling for Ellen to run a hot bath. Ellen was there in an instant, fussing and tut-tutting as her mother never had.

Once more she said, 'I'm OK, Byrne.' But she didn't mind at all that he continued to hold her while the water swished and bubbled in the tub, while the room filled with steam and wrapped them in the soothing aroma of fragrant lavender.

'I got everything you ordered,' Ellen told Byrne. 'Shampoo, lotions, soaps, bath salts.' And then she hurried back to the kitchen, mumbling something about dinner in the oven.

Byrne lowered Fiona gently to a Bentwood chair. 'Stay in here and soak for as long as you like. Let the bath salts relax your muscles.'

'I feel such a baby.'

He shook his head, touched his thumb to her cheek. 'I should have known better. I kept you out for too long and worked you too hard.' The pad of his thumb traced the curve of her cheek, his touch so gentle she almost wept. And then, 'Do you need a hand to get undressed?'

She looked up to see a playful, sexy smile she'd never expected from the dour Byrne Drummond and, in spite of her aching body, she felt a sweep of sweet longing flow through her.

'I'll manage on my own, thank you.' She sent him a 'watch your step' look, more because it was expected than because she really wanted him to leave.

He did leave, however, but as his tall, rangy figure disappeared through the doorway she knew she was in trouble. Deep trouble.

'Byrne.'

Her voice brought him wheeling around, like a cattle dog responding to a ringer's whistle.

'I think I'm going to need your help to get my boots off.'

Byrne's throat and chest tightened. And at the thought of going back in that bathroom the tightness sped south.

It had been bad enough when he'd been in there before, thinking about Fiona undressing and getting into the bath, but he'd escaped in the nick of time. Stepping back through the doorway now, he felt punch-drunk, like a boxer bravely heading back into the ring for the final knockout.

She was still sitting where he'd left her, except that one booted foot was resting on the edge of the bath. Her face was pale and framed by curling tendrils of hair, dampened by the steam rising from the bath.

'I'm sorry,' she said. 'I can't manage the boots.'

'No problem.' Without letting his gaze meet hers, he knelt and performed the task for her, gently easing the ankle-high, elastic-sided boots and then removing her socks. And he found himself staring at her pink feet, neat and dainty. Like her hands. She would be neat and dainty all over.

He swallowed and stood quickly, swallowed again. 'You'll be all right with your jeans?'

Fiona forced a weak grin. 'I'm sure I'll manage them.'

She inched her bottom from the chair, tried to stand and winced.

'Here, lean on me.' Byrne's voice was gruff but he supported her while she stood straight. He knew she was going to need help with those jeans. No doubt about it.

Best to get it over quickly.

Keeping his gaze hard, his face in a set frown, he reached down and unsnapped the fastener on her jeans with a brisk, businesslike action, then lowered the zip. There was a flash of her creamy skin and white silk undies, but he willed himself not to show any flicker of interest as he slid the denim down over her soft, round thighs, past her knees and her shapely calves.

He felt the pressure of her hands on his shoulders as she let him take her weight, while she freed her feet from the bottoms of the jeans, murmuring her thanks.

Wanting, needing to feast his eyes on her, he snatched his gaze away and drew a long, shaky breath as he stared at the green and white ceramic tiles around the bath, then stood.

A brief glance found Fiona's green eyes watching him.

'You should be all right with the rest?'

'Yes. Absolutely.' Her voice was small, sounding choked.

He turned, and as he left he caught a brief glimpse of her standing beside the bath, wearing nothing but her pale pink shirt, crumpled from being tucked inside her jeans and skimming the tops of her thighs.

Without another word, he got the hell out of there.

It was completely dark when Fiona woke.

At first she couldn't think where she was, and had to study the unfamiliar room lit faintly by starlight—saw a plain little Baltic-pine chest of drawers, filmy white curtains and a row of old-fashioned, five-paned casement windows, and framed wildflowers in cross-stitch on the wall.

And everything came back to her.

Falling asleep in the bath, being woken by the house-keeper's discreet tap on the door, too sore to get out of the bath without Ellen's help, too tired to eat dinner. Stumbling here to the spare bedroom at Coolaroo, swathed in a luxurious, towelling bathrobe. The sheer bliss of clean sheets, a soft, plump pillow sprinkled with lavender water and a silk nightdress in the prettiest shade of pale apricot, a new hairbrush and comb.

'Byrne sent me into Gundawarra to buy all these things for you,' Ellen had confided. 'Such a long list he gave me. But you need them all, poor love.'

So kind of Byrne. So surprising.

Fiona moved a little now, testing her body to see how much it ached. Lying still in one position had only served to make her stiffness worse.

Her stomach growled, and she realised she was hungry. Not merely hungry—ravenous. She'd missed dinner, and lunch, a corned meat sandwich and another mug of black billy tea, had been hours and hours ago. She wondered how much it would hurt if she tried to roll out of bed and shuffle out to the kitchen to rustle up a snack.

There was a sound in the hall outside her room. A footstep. And then a tall, shadowy figure in the doorway.

She inched up on her elbows, her heart thrumming. 'Byrne, is that you?'

'I thought I'd check to make sure you were OK,' he said, taking a step into the room, into the pearl-grey starlight that filtered through the curtains.

'What time is it?' she asked, suddenly breathless to have him so close to her bed.

'Not late. Around eleven. The others have gone to bed. Are you hungry?'

'Yes, I am, actually. I was just about to investigate the kitchen.'

'You should stay there. I'll bring you something on a tray.'

She pushed her sheets aside, looked around for the bath robe. 'No, Byrne, you've done enough.'

'Stay there.' It was a command. 'Ellen left something prepared. She guessed you might get hungry in the middle of the night. It just needs a zap in the microwave.' He turned to leave.

'Byrne,' she called softly as he reached the doorway. 'Thank you. For everything. You've been so thoughtful, sending Ellen into town to buy things for me.' She touched the thin ribboned strap of her nightgown. 'This is lovely.'

Despite the shadows, she could see the gleam in his eyes as he smiled. 'It certainly is.'

Then he disappeared, but he was back in a matter

of minutes with a tray that he set on top of the chest of drawers.

'That's wonderful,' she said, and she expected him to leave her, but he remained close to the edge of the bed.

He looked so intensely desirable she could hardly breathe. It wasn't just his height and broad shoulders and dark good looks. There was something else, an elemental, very primal and compelling power in Byrne that she'd never sensed in any other man.

Her body reacted as if he'd caressed her. A coil of longing flowered low inside her, and an unbearable tension tightened her breasts, making them strain against the silk of her nightgown.

Byrne sat on the edge of the bed, and her heart went wild, performing a string of cartwheels.

'How are you feeling now?' he asked softly.

Um… Breathless… More than a little lust-crazed.

'Still stiff and sore, but I think I'll live.'

'You'll probably never want to get back on another horse.'

'Well, maybe not tomorrow.'

They shared a smile in the starlight, and Fiona wondered if she was dreaming.

Was this really the taciturn, disdainful Byrne Drummond looking at her with unmistakeable tenderness, with the same yearning she felt for him?

His right hand lay dark against the white sheet, mere inches from her thigh.

Could he guess how she felt, that she was falling in love with him?

So burning up that she thought she might explode, she

brushed the tips of her fingers against the edge of his hand, the merest feather-soft contact of skin against skin.

It was enough.

She felt fine tremors pass through him and then, with a soft groan, he leaned over her, touched his lips to hers.

Her body tightened all over, her skin turned to flames as he took his weight on his elbows, as if he was afraid of hurting her, and allowed only their soft, open mouths to touch.

It was the most astonishing, tantalising kiss she'd ever experienced. Within seconds, she was a trembling mass of need.

She'd been waiting so long for this, had been thinking of little else for days now. Unable to hold back, she wrapped her arms around his neck and arched up to him in a shameless gesture of offering.

His attempts at gentleness flew out the window.

Passion claimed them both and their kiss turned hungry, a wild mating of lips, tongues and teeth. Byrne's big hands skimmed her sides, exploring her shape beneath the silky nightdress. His palms smoothed her bare shoulders, his lips pressed heated kisses into the hot curve of her neck. His thumbs traced the lines of her collar bones.

She wanted to touch him, too, and she dragged at his shirt, pulling it free from his jeans. Her hands trembled as she felt his skin beneath the shirt burning smooth and taut. Palms spread, she explored his hard chest muscles, and the smattering of dark, springy hair, let her fingertips graze his nipples.

With a choked groan, he hooked his thumbs beneath the straps of her nightgown.

'I can't believe you're this beautiful,' he whispered as he eased the gown down and lowered his lips to her breasts.

A cry burst from her as desire, hot and miraculous, flooded her. Her hips bucked with frantic need and her legs twined around his.

Then she let out a yelp as her muscles cramped. Painfully.

Byrne pulled away. 'I'm sorry,' he said. 'I didn't mean to hurt you. I—I forgot.'

'I'm OK,' she said, desperately reaching a hand around his neck and nuzzling the rugged line of his jaw. 'You can't hurt me. It's just muscle cramp.'

At the worst possible moment.

Shaking his head, Byrne took her hands in both of his and lifted them away from him. 'I'm sorry. I got carried away.'

'I'm ever so grateful that you did,' she whispered.

He smiled softly, lifted the straps of her gown back to her shoulders, then pinned her hands by her sides and kissed her again, on the lips, very gently, in an echo of the way their kiss had started. She kissed him back as passionately as he would allow, but already he was drawing further away from her.

'I didn't offer you refuge in my home so I could ravish you,' he said.

'What a pity,' she couldn't help replying. 'You ravish so very beautifully.'

He stood, and she saw amusement flicker in his face. 'You should eat your supper before it gets cold.'

* * *

Much later, after Byrne had left and she had eaten her supper, Fiona lay awake, too excited to sleep. She knew now, without doubt, that she was deeply in love with Byrne. She had never met a man like him, had never felt this astonishing depth of connection before, couldn't imagine her life without him.

And she knew that even if his kiss meant nothing more to him than light flirtation, even if he could never return her love, she would be marked for ever.

Standing at his bedroom window, Byrne stared out into the dark bush, while behind him his abandoned bed and tangled sheets were a testament to his restlessness.

Fiona was driving him crazy and he wasn't quite sure what to do about it. His thoughts chased each other, ducking, diving and weaving, like a flock of mischievous swallows.

It was no use pretending that he wasn't madly attracted to her. And the signals she'd given suggested she was attracted to him. Each time he'd come close to her, each time he'd been honest to his innermost feelings and kissed her, he'd uncovered a passion and sensuality as gut-tumbling and deep as his own.

That kind of chemistry was hard to dismiss.

But what should he do about it? What did he want?

Everyone, including his mother and his friends, assured him it was time to 'get a life'. And that, he knew, was poorly disguised code for 'get a woman'.

Mitch Layton had tried to talk about it. 'Admit it, Byrne, you're a man who needs a woman in your life.'

He'd told poor Mitch to take a flying leap, to mind his own business.

But he sensed that his mates foresaw a bleak future for him as a sad and pathetic figure, hiding behind the façade of not wanting or needing a woman. He sighed deeply, turned away from the window and back to the empty bed.

The wife he'd loved had died three years ago and she would never come back to him.

Three years, close on a thousand days…and nights.

Did he really think he'd manage alone indefinitely? Could he honestly expect to spend the rest of his thirties, forties, fifties and beyond without needing the company or the intimacy of a woman?

CHAPTER NINE

WHEN Fiona wandered into the kitchen next morning, she was surprised to find that Riley had already left for school and Ellen and Ted had disappeared to attend to daily chores. Byrne, however, was still sitting at the table, drinking coffee.

One glance at the warm light in his eyes and she felt pinpricks of excitement, as if she'd been bombarded with tiny darts. She prayed that she didn't blush.

'Good afternoon,' he said, smiling. 'I trust you slept well?'

'Very well,' she lied. 'And you?'

He grinned and dropped his gaze to his coffee cup. 'I've slept better.'

A secret thrill rippled through her. He'd been as restless as she had after he'd left her room.

'How are the muscles today?' he asked.

'Wonderful. Good as new.'

'Liar.'

She shrugged and smiled. 'OK, they're still pretty sore, but I'll mend.'

From her bedroom behind her came the shrill ring of her mobile phone.

Byrne looked at her expectantly. 'Don't you want to answer that?'

'Not much point,' she said, heading for the coffee pot and filling a mug with the strong, aromatic brew. 'My phone's battery is low, and no one can hear me because it keeps breaking up. And I can't re-charge it because the adaptor cord burned in the fire.'

'You're welcome to ring your office and give them our number.'

'Thanks. I'll probably have to do that.' She smiled at him over the rim of her coffee cup. 'But I'll do it later. No rush. After all, it's about time the office managed without me. I'm supposed to be on leave.'

After a quick check of the bread box on the kitchen counter, she held up one of Ellen's home-made cob loaves. 'All right if I help myself?'

'Of course, by all means.' Byrne jumped to his feet, and looked embarrassed that he'd forgotten his duties as her host. 'Can I slice that for you?'

'No thanks. I'll manage.' She found a bread knife, cut a neat enough slice and popped it into the toaster, then leaned back against the kitchen counter, sipping coffee while she waited.

'Your business seems rather high-pressured,' Byrne said.

She nodded. 'It's getting busier all the time.'

Her toast popped up, and she found a plate and knife, carried them and the coffee to the table, and sat opposite him.

As he watched her spread butter on her toast, he said, 'I know next to nothing about your work.'

'That's probably a good thing. I doubt it would interest you.'

'Why wouldn't I be interested?'

Surprised, she looked up.

He smiled. 'I'm interested in you, Fiona. I'd like to know more.'

A tiny pulse began to beat at the base of her throat.

Byrne settled back in his chair, as if he was ready to give her his full attention.

More flattered by his interest than she cared to admit, Fiona helped herself to marmalade, cut her toast and took a small bite.

'You're high up in the marketing world,' he said. 'Is that right?'

'Yes.'

'How did you get started?'

She frowned. 'You really want to know?'

'Yes.'

It was the truth. She could see it in his eyes.

Trying not to look too pleased, she pressed her finger onto a toast crumb and popped it in her mouth. 'I first started working at a lifestyle magazine called *Urban Life*—selling advertising for restaurants, wineries, inner-city property developers. And I became really interested in things like branding and imaging, so I headed off to university and majored in communications and marketing.'

She ate a little more of her toast.

'After I graduated I had an amazing lucky break. Rex

Hartley picked me up. At the time, his business was pretty much old-world style, dealing mainly with black and white newspaper ads. I think he saw me as the gateway to the next generation, and after only a couple of years he made me a junior partner. I was over the moon.'

'Junior partner,' Byrne repeated, and his eyes widened. 'Hartley must have really valued you.'

'He liked the fact that I had youth and vitality and fresh ideas, but I also understood the importance of bottom-line returns. I seemed to have an ability to pick what was going to work and what was likely to fail.'

'And you were happy to work with him?'

'Of course. Rex is very highly respected in the industry. He has the kind of esteem that can only be earned after years and years of honest work. He and I make a good team. Rex trusts my judgement and I respect the reputation he's built. His good name.'

'He's an older man?'

She nodded. 'Another reason I like working with him. I really don't like a lot of the younger guys in marketing. You know, buttons undone, professional highlights in their hair, metrosexuals.'

It was on the tip of her tongue to add that she preferred men like him. Country guys were unpretentious, manly in every old-fashioned sense of the word.

But Byrne jumped in with another question. 'What's your company called?'

'Hartley & McLaren.' She grinned at him. 'Referred to by those in the know as "H and M".'

His right eyebrow took a hike.

'We have some big accounts. Government departments, the postal service, defence force recruiting, mining.'

Sensing growing tension in Byrne, Fiona quickly changed tack. 'But there's a downside. I haven't taken a holiday for at least five years. I've hardly been out of Sydney unless it was to go to a seminar or a conference.'

To her dismay, she realised that the light-heartedness in Byrne's face had vanished to be replaced by a sombre, wary look.

'And you're supposed to be on holiday now?' he said.

'Yes. I had to make a decision about White Cliffs, and Rex could see that I was worried, so he urged me to take some extended leave to sort this out. I'm under orders to enjoy myself while I'm here.'

'I suppose that's why you went to the Gundawarra ball.'

His comment, coming from left field, surprised her. Their gazes locked, and she knew he was remembering the night at the ball. She was remembering it, too, remembering their kiss and the angry aftermath and all that had happened since, including their second, mindblowing kiss last night.

Byrne dropped his gaze to his hands clasped on the table top in front of him.

'It hasn't been much of a holiday for you. You haven't had much fun.'

She shrugged. 'Holidays are wasted on me. I'm not very good at relaxing. If you dumped me on a tropical island, I'd probably draw up a marketing plan for coconuts.'

His response was a small, mirthless smile and then

his chair slid back as he stood. 'It's never too late to learn new habits. You should take it very easy today. Put your feet up. Read a book. Take more warm baths.'

She tried not to mind that their friendly interlude had come to an end and that Byrne was clearly planning to desert her. It seemed rather obvious that she'd disappointed him somehow. After all, he'd hung around especially to chat with her. *I'm interested in you, Fiona.* But, as soon as she'd told him everything, he seemed less than happy. Disillusioned?

'What are your plans for today?' she asked.

'I've organized for a team to come across from Tilba to start work on your fences.' He glanced at the kitchen wall-clock. 'They should be here soon. So I'd better head off.'

Riley's happy giggles were the first thing that greeted Byrne when he entered the homestead that evening. Curious, he headed straight for the living room and found Fiona and Riley stretched out on the carpet, playing dominoes. Other board games were scattered on the floor beside them—snakes and ladders, Chinese chequers, draughts.

At the sound of his footsteps, Fiona looked up; her green eyes, already alight with laughter, burned brighter when she saw him, and he felt emotion slam into him, then slide low.

'You look like you're having fun.'

'We are, Daddy.' Scamp jumped up to hug him. 'We've played so many games. And Fiona's taught me stretches.'

'Stretches?'

'Muscle stretches,' Fiona supplied. 'Ones I've learned at dance classes.'

His gaze slid over her slim, lithe body clad in the T-shirt and soft track-pants that Ellen had bought yesterday. 'How are the aches and pains now?'

She pulled a face. 'Still pretty fierce.'

He nodded and knew that he should leave them to their games. He'd spent the day reminding himself of the inescapable reality that Fiona McLaren was a high-powered city woman, not right for him in any shape or form. Which was why he should have turned on his heel and taken a shower, a cold shower.

Instead he dropped to his haunches beside Fiona and said, 'You need a massage.'

Closing her eyes, she released a soft, purring sigh. 'Oh, I'd pay anything for a good massage.'

'No need.' He placed a hand, a surprisingly steady hand, on her shoulder. 'This one's free.'

Awareness leapt in her eyes like erect green flames, but was quickly replaced by a smile so sweet that a rock jammed his throat.

Rolling onto her stomach, she murmured, 'I'm very gratefully at your tender mercy.'

'What are you doing, Daddy?'

He'd almost forgotten that Riley was there, observing his every move with round, curious eyes.

Byrne cleared his throat. *'I'm rubbing Fiona's sore back and legs.' And trying to ignore how fabulous she looks and how incredibly feminine and soft she feels.*

'Can I help?'

'Sure.'

Thank you, kiddo, you'll keep this scenario safe.

'Be very gentle, now.'

At that, Fiona sent him a sly, cheeky grin, and he felt another thrust of desire.

How crazy was this? He was supposed to be remembering this morning's conversation, remembering that there was no future for him and this woman. He shouldn't be here, touching her, making out that he was trying to help her aching muscles.

Step back, mate.

From now on he had to be extra careful. Once dinner was over, he'd find an excuse to make himself scarce. Mend the tractor. Anything that kept him out of the house, out of the danger zone, any place where his eyes were not going to meet this woman's.

Byrne kept another day's careful distance from Fiona. He didn't even enquire how she planned to fill in her day, and several surprises awaited him when he returned to Coolaroo the next evening shortly before sunset.

The first was that Ted's ute was missing. He felt a moment's alarm. Had there been an emergency requiring a rushed trip into town?

The second surprise was the smell wafting from the kitchen as he crossed the verandah, a very Italian aroma redolent with garlic, tomatoes and herbs, not Ellen's usual fare. His alarm deepened.

And then he heard sounds. Feminine laughter. Jazz piano music. Riley's voice, bubbly and high-pitched with excitement.

He reached the kitchen door.

Fiona, her autumn hair bundled into a haphazard knot and swathed in one of Ellen's enormous floral aprons, was at the stove, stirring something in a huge pot with a wooden spoon. Riley, wearing her favourite pink T-shirt and frothy ballet tutu, and with her brown hair neatly secured into some kind of fancy bun, was perched on a high stool, giggling as she snapped the ends from beans.

They both turned when he came into the room, their faces rosy with warmth from steaming cooking pots and their eyes sparkling with gaiety.

'What's going on here?' By now he was almost certain that something had happened to Ellen. But surely Fiona and Riley wouldn't have looked quite so relaxed and happy?

'Hi, Daddy.' Scamp waved and beamed a grin at him. 'Fiona and me are cooking dinner.'

'Where's Ellen?'

'She's having a night off,' said Fiona. 'There's a movie, a romantic comedy, showing in Gundawarra and Ellen let slip that she really wanted to see it. So she and Ted have gone to town. They're having dinner first at Rosita's café.'

Byrne scratched the back of his neck, suddenly bemused by this unexpected turn of events.

'We're having s'ghetti,' Riley announced. 'And I've made a special dessert all by myself, but I'm not telling you what it is, Daddy. It's a secret.'

His little girl was almost bursting with pride.

'Well, now,' he said. 'Looks like I'm in for an exciting night.'

'How did the fencing go?' Fiona asked.

'We made steady progress.' Suddenly conscious of being hot and dusty after a day working in the outdoors, he looked down at his grubby jeans. 'If you'll excuse me, I'll go and take a shower and get ready for this feast.'

'Just a minute, Daddy.'

Riley's face was glowing with happiness as she scrambled down from the stool. 'Look at me.' She twirled in front of him in a fair imitation of a pirouette.

'Wow.'

'I look like a proper ballerina, don't I?' She patted the top of her head. 'Fiona did my hair up in a bun.'

'You look very swish.'

'An' Fiona taught me ballet. Watch me, Daddy.'

Her little face became a portrait in concentration as she stood very straight with her heels together, toes out and her plump little arms curved above her head. Then, with a fierce effort of concentration, she gave a little jump and one foot came forward, toe pointed with excruciating care, then another jump, and the action was reversed with the other foot forward now.

She looked up at him, brown eyes radiant. 'That's proper ballet.'

Byrne felt his throat tighten. 'It certainly is, sweetheart. You look beautiful, just like a real ballerina.'

His glance flew to Fiona, who was still standing at the stove, watching them intently. 'It's her heart's desire to become a ballerina,' he said. 'But it's hard to get her into town for lessons.'

Fiona smiled. 'I know exactly how she feels. It was all I wanted at her age, too. But I couldn't take dancing lessons till I was an adult and earning my own money.'

Suddenly he was remembering Fiona at the ball. She'd told him then that she danced to keep fit. He remembered how surprisingly well they had danced together, how light and fluid Fiona had been in his arms, making him feel like Fred Astaire.

As he showered, he was buffeted by see-sawing emotions. A fierce possessive love for Riley. And happiness, too, to see her so excited. But there was also a pang of jealousy. His little girl and Fiona were related by blood, whereas he, Riley's father, was an outsider, usurping a role handed to him by fate.

But, just as quickly as it had flared, his jealousy was replaced by his desire for Fiona.

But what was the point in that? He was a fool to think that way about her—a city businesswoman, out of his reach.

Just now, however, in his kitchen with Scamp, she'd looked so at home, so available.

That thought was enough to make him turn off the hot tap and drench himself in cold water.

Reaching for a towel, however, he had to admit that he felt more than desire for Fiona. He'd come to respect her, to enjoy her company, her friendship, and to feel an unexpected tenderness.

How neat and tidy it would be if he married her. Riley would have a mother again, a woman who understood all the needs of a little girl in ways he never could. Instead of looking ahead to years of loneliness, he would have companionship, a partner, a lover.

For a full minute he allowed a picture of their

marriage to take hold. He saw Fiona in his bed night and morning, Fiona riding beside him as they envisioned a new future for the properties of White Cliffs and Coolaroo, Fiona becoming deeply involved in Riley's life. He could even imagine the possibility of another child or two, and he felt a leap of excitement so fierce, he almost let out a whoop of joy.

But then, with the chilling swiftness of a falling axe, he remembered it was not going to happen.

Brutal reality sank home, leaving him with nothing but the painful truth. He was attracted to Fiona, fiercely, irrevocably.

And she was just as fiercely and irrevocably unavailable.

She wasn't just any city woman; she was a super-important, famously competent business-whiz in high demand in the corporate world, a flaming junior partner in Hartley and bloody McLaren.

Only a man with rocks in his head could think a woman like that would sacrifice everything she'd worked so hard to achieve to bury herself in the country with him.

He'd been a prime fool to give the idea a second thought.

By the time he'd changed into clean jeans and a fresh white shirt for dinner, he'd made up his mind. He couldn't, under any circumstances, expect Fiona to marry him. But he was reasonably confident that she might be interested in an affair.

It would be better than nothing. He could be her holiday fling and in the future they might get together for an occasional liaison.

He could almost imagine her telling her sophisticated city friends that he was her 'country interest', her 'sometimes significant other'.

It wasn't a role he accepted gladly. But, under the circumstances, it was the best he could hope for.

In the kitchen, Fiona had covered the table with a dark red cloth and set it with the Drummonds' best silver and finest white bone-china. She'd set fine white candles in silver candlesticks, and red and white roses in a cut-glass vase.

'Excuse me,' Byrne said. 'I think I've come home to the wrong house.'

Riley giggled.

And Fiona flushed, offered him an apologetic smile. 'We got carried away with a party mood,' she said.

She'd removed Ellen's apron to reveal a simply stunning little black dress, and she looked so incredibly lovely he couldn't help throwing his arm around her shoulders and dropping a quick kiss on her forehead.

'A party is a great idea,' he said, and he let his eyes travel over her dress. It hugged the enticing curves of her breasts and her slim waist and bottom perfectly. 'Don't tell me you found this little number in Gundawarra.'

'I did, actually. In Marguerite's salon. She has some lovely things.' She managed to look guilty. 'But I hope you're not expecting a really fancy meal, Byrne. I'm afraid it's only spaghetti Bolognese.' She nodded her head towards Riley. 'My apprentice chose the menu.'

'It smells fabulous.'

And he discovered very soon that Fiona's cooking tasted fabulous, too. 'You didn't get this out of a bottle.'

'No,' she admitted. 'I have an Italian friend who taught me her family's ancient recipe.'

'What's the secret?'

'Loads of tomatoes and only a little meat.' She smiled at him as she deftly twirled strands of spaghetti around her fork.

'And garlic,' added Scamp importantly. 'Fiona smashed garlic with the side of a knife and she pressed it into a little hill of salt.'

'And I threw in lots of herbs.'

Riley nodded. 'Handfuls and handfuls of herbs.'

'Handfuls and handfuls?'

Fiona laughed, and her green eyes flashed happily in the candlelight. 'One or two handfuls.'

Byrne thought of the pot-luck dinners he'd had at the Laytons', of his circle of friends all laughing and enjoying simple meals in each other's company, and he allowed himself to imagine taking Fiona to an evening like that. His friends would really like her. Better still, he would love to host a dinner here, with her help.

Whoa, there. He was getting carried away again. That little scenario was never going to happen.

'Is something the matter?' Fiona was looking at him, her eyes shadowed with concern.

He gave a little shake and smiled. 'Not at all.'

But he knew he hadn't convinced her, and he felt like a heel for spoiling the mood.

'Is it time for dessert?' Riley asked, deflecting Fiona's attention and saving the moment.

He and Riley had eaten everything on their plates and Fiona had almost finished.

Fiona winked at Riley. 'Yes, it's time for your special surprise.'

His daughter and Fiona retreated to the far corner of the kitchen to huddle in a whispered conversation that he knew he wasn't supposed to hear.

'Wouldn't you like to serve something with your jelly?' Fiona was asking. 'Sliced peaches? Or ice cream? Ice cream tastes great with jelly.'

'No.' Riley insisted. 'I didn't make the ice cream. I just want to give Daddy jelly. That's what I made.'

Moments later, her little face contorted with the effort of swallowing a proud grin, she walked back to the table carrying a bowl of bright green jelly.

'Good heavens,' Byrne exclaimed as she set it carefully in front of him. 'You didn't make this all by yourself, did you?'

Riley nodded, danced a jig of excited anticipation. 'Try it, Daddy.'

He was not and never had been a fan of jelly, but Riley's brown eyes watched every movement as he carefully lifted his spoon, scooped a piece of wobbling green jelly and ate it.

'Wow. This is magnificent, Scamp. The finest jelly I've ever tasted.'

'I'm going to make it for you every night,' she announced, grinning blissfully.

Fiona was nervous as she tidied the kitchen and stacked the dishwasher, while Byrne got Riley ready for bed. She knew that the dinner, the candles and the little black dress had made it screamingly obvious that she was trying to impress Byrne. She might as well have hung a cardboard sign around her neck: *Take me. I'm yours.*

She knew he'd been avoiding her and she'd finally guessed the reason: she'd frightened him off when she'd told him about her job. So now it was important to show him that she wasn't merely a city businesswoman, that his home, his daughter and his considerable masculine appeal had awoken other needs in her.

Over the past few weeks her life back in the city had felt less and less real. And now she'd arrived at a conclusion that had been utterly unreachable till now: her career at Hartley & McLaren had been an interesting chapter in her life, an exciting interlude in her twenties, but nothing more.

It was almost as if her entire city career had been a pleasant way to fill in time till she discovered what she *really* wanted to do with her life. And now she was quietly but unshakably confident that her destiny lay here. At Coolaroo with Byrne Drummond.

The obvious measures she'd taken this evening, the black dress, the table set with candles, were quite out of character. Normally, she was very cautious with men, playing her cards close to her chest.

In the city she'd learned the hard way that men were attracted to women in positions of power, but all they wanted was to have sex and then boast about it. She had no interest in being anybody's trophy, and she'd perfected the art of turning men away without bruising their precious egos, mainly because she needed their egos intact for boardroom negotiations.

She'd met nice guys, of course. At university she'd had a steady boyfriend who'd been very sweet, but when they'd graduated they'd gone their separate ways. He'd been much keener to settle down than she was and he'd virtually married the next girl he'd met.

A couple of years ago, she'd met a very amusing and charming guy at a conference in Singapore, a Danish divorcee with no intention of settling down. He'd had a marvellous sense of humour. They'd really hit it off, and had stayed on in Singapore for a few extra days. But, when they'd gone their separate ways, her heart hadn't broken.

There'd been others, but none had really sent her pulse racing.

None of the men in her past had the raw and rugged masculine appeal Byrne had. None had touched her heart or stirred her senses till she could think of nothing but him and how much she needed him. None had inspired her to completely reassess her life, her goals.

'I don't think I've ever seen my little girl quite so happy.'

She'd been so lost in her thoughts that she hadn't heard him return, and the sound of his voice in the doorway startled her. The cup she'd been putting in the dishwasher slipped from her hand and the handle broke off.

'Sorry,' Byrne said, coming further into the room. 'I didn't mean to startle you.'

'I was in another world,' she confessed. Crouching low, she fished for the handle that had fallen right to the bottom of the dishwasher. When she retrieved it she held the cup up. 'I hope this wasn't valuable.'

'I've no idea.' Byrne shrugged and smiled. 'It doesn't matter. I'll put the damage on your bill.'

She knew he was joking, but he'd raised a point she couldn't overlook. 'You've been so kind to let me stay here. That's one of the reasons I wanted to cook dinner.'

He leaned a hip against a cupboard and watched as she set the broken mug on the draining board, rinsed her hands, and dried them on a towel. 'I don't think I've ever eaten such great Bolognese. Did your Italian friend teach you any other recipes?'

Folding her arms over her chest, she lifted an eyebrow and flashed him a pert smile. 'I make a mean lasagne. And perfect pesto.'

'I'm salivating at the thought.'

'I have Greek, Vietnamese and Thai friends, too.'

'Don't tell me they've all given you cooking tips?'

'Indeed.'

Fiona's bright smile wavered. Despite the lightness of their conversation and Byrne's casual pose, she sensed an edginess in him as tense as her own. She knew neither of them really wanted to talk about cooking. 'Would you like some coffee?'

'No thanks.'

Her arms tightened across her chest. 'Is Riley asleep?'

'Almost.'

Across the kitchen, her green eyes and his grey shared a look, a glittering, charged exchange. Byrne took a step towards her, and her insides began to clamour like bells on Christmas morning. She let her hands fall to her sides, and Byrne took another step closer and he reached for them. Her skin jumped and prickled.

'You do realise that I'm going to have to kiss you again, don't you?'

Her heart was beating in her throat now and she tried to cover her mounting excitement with a gentle tease. 'A third kiss, Byrne?'

He smiled. 'Who's counting?'

She blushed, looked away.

But he took pity on her. 'A third kiss is significant, isn't it?'

Fighting a strong urge to hurl herself into his arms, she said lightly, 'I'm sure it is, especially if the three kisses occur on three separate occasions.'

'Our first kiss was merely a playful adventure,' he said. 'A pirate and a butterfly. I had no idea who was behind that mask.' He spoke easily, but there was a deep, husky edge to his voice betraying a tension as brittle as hers. 'I suppose the second kiss was experimental.'

'The other night was an experiment?' She pretended to be shocked.

'But a third kiss.' He pulled her close, so close she could smell the faint, elusive hint of his cologne. 'A third kiss is...'

'Dangerous?'

He didn't laugh, was too intent on drawing her hard against him, too focused on tasting her. 'Compulsory,' he murmured as his lips covered hers.

CHAPTER TEN

THEIR third kiss was beyond wonderful, deep and ardent, breathtaking in its sensual promise.

But it was not enough.

Both Fiona and Byrne knew, almost as soon as their lips met, that this kiss would be a mere prelude to deeper intimacy. They were too on fire, their bodies too tense, their skin too burning with the need to kiss more than each other's lips, to touch more. This time there could be no holding back.

'I wonder if Scamp's asleep yet?' Byrne whispered hoarsely.

'Let's check.'

Holding hands, their hearts racing and their cheeks hot, they tiptoed breathlessly down the carpeted hallway.

Byrne had left a small lamp glowing on Riley's bedside table and by its rose-gold light they saw the little girl curled on her side, eyes shut as she cuddled two tattered, much loved toys. She was wearing frilly pink pyjamas, looked sweet and rosy, and Fiona felt a distinctly maternal pang.

Riley really was the cutest little button and they'd had the loveliest times together.

'She's mad about you,' Byrne said softly, and his fingers squeezed Fiona's.

'Ditto,' she whispered. And then she looked again at the faded toys with their patches of missing fur. A small yellow bear and a rather ugly green-and-brown-striped dinosaur. 'Those toys aren't Athengar and, um—?'

'Dunkum?'

'Dunkum. Yes.'

'The same,' he said softly. 'She won't sleep unless she has them both.'

Fiona stared at the sleeping child in astonishment. There were other toys in the room, a little cradle, pretty dolls, a plush, pink rabbit and a lavender unicorn. It was hard to believe that the toy she'd grabbed so hastily on that fateful day three and a bit years ago could have been so faithfully loved.

Then she realised that Riley had opened her eyes and was squinting up at them. She blinked and looked straight at Fiona, her brown eyes suddenly huge and shining with suppressed excitement.

'Was it you?' she asked.

'Me?'

'Were you the pretty lady who brought me Athengar?'

Fiona was so shocked her heart seemed to fill her throat, and she could barely whisper. 'Yes. Do you remember?'

Riley nodded solemnly.

How could the child remember? She'd been only three at the time. She'd been in a terrible accident, was concussed. Her mother had just died.

The little girl's features softened and she smiled, a smile as warm and pretty as a sunrise. 'I'm so glad it was you, Fiona.'

Tears slipped down Fiona's cheeks, and she felt Byrne's arms tighten around her shoulders. Looking up, she saw that his eyes were suspiciously damp.

He blinked, bent down and kissed his little girl's forehead. 'Now go back to sleep.'

Riley snuggled down obediently, hugged the toys close. 'Night, Daddy. Night, Fiona.' She smiled with her eyes tightly shut.

'I'm going to turn out your light now,' Byrne said. 'OK?'

'OK.'

They left the room, holding hands. In silence, Byrne led Fiona further down the passage to the far corner of the house. To his room.

Filmy white curtains fluttered over two sets of French doors opening onto front and side verandahs. Through one set of doors, Fiona could see the moon riding high, sailing through a layer of hazy clouds.

Stopping in the middle of the big room, Byrne held her hands lightly and looked at her with such a mixture of tenderness and desire that she couldn't breathe. Then he drew her into a fierce embrace, buried his face in her hair, his chest heaving with deep emotion.

'I'm sorry,' he whispered against her cheek.

'Sorry, Byrne? Why?'

'I've done everything I could to keep you and Riley apart. I was wrong. Crazy with jealousy.'

With shaking fingers, she touched his cheek and discovered tears. Her heart broke for him. 'You were perfectly justified.'

His sigh was a desperate hush. Turning his face just a little, he pressed warm kisses into the inner curve of her palm.

She let her head rest against the solid bulk of his shoulder. 'I can't believe Riley remembers that day,' she said. 'I can't actually remember why I bought that toy. Except that I felt I owed her something, and I'd seen you with Dunkum.'

She looked up, her vision blurred. 'You didn't know I was watching you, Byrne, but I saw you when you first arrived in the hospital's emergency ward. You were still wearing your oilskin coat, and you looked so shocked and bereft. You were clutching that little toy bear and I was so moved. I don't think I'll ever forget that picture of you for as long as I live.'

He kissed the tip of her nose. 'I remember you looked damn sexy in your business suit.' He sighed again, and she felt his breath fan her skin. 'At the time I thought I hated you. How could I have been so wrong?'

She wasn't sure what to say, wished she was brave enough to admit that she loved him, but was glad that he kissed her instead.

It was a tender kiss, tasting faintly of salty tears, a kiss trembling with an overspill of emotion, sharing secrets deeper than words.

There was no rush now. They savoured the slow, lush commingling, enjoyed the luxury of letting their desire rebuild, allowing their kisses to deepen from tender to demanding, while their caresses grew more daring, more feverish and thrilling.

When, at last, they'd tempted each other beyond bearing, Byrne slid down the zipper on Fiona's dress and lifted the whispering fabric over her head. There was a momentary beat in time when she saw his face, saw his desire unmasked as he let his gaze rest on her.

And then they were in each other's arms again, laughing a little, stealing kisses as they helped each other out of the rest of their clothing.

'About those aches and pains of yours,' Byrne murmured.

'What about them?'

For answer, he slipped one arm around her shoulders and another behind her knees, scooped her up and carried her to the bed.

'You're going to need another massage,' he said as he laid her down gently.

His hands rode gently over her bare thighs, spreading shivery heat wherever he touched.

'I most definitely need another massage,' she murmured huskily, sinking fast beneath the spell of his touch. 'I'm aching everywhere, Byrne. All over.'

Some time past midnight, Fiona stirred, gently lifted Byrne's arm and tried to slip away without disturbing him. She didn't want to leave, but felt she must. But as her feet reached the floor Byrne's hand caught her wrist.

'You're not running away, are you?'

'I was going back to my room.'

'Why?'

She looked back at him, saw the strong planes of his face in the moonlight, and her heart flipped. 'You don't want Riley to find me here in the morning.'

He tugged gently on her wrist. 'I want you here, Fiona.'

'But—'

'Don't worry,' he murmured. 'I'm always up before Scamp. She won't come in here.' His fingers traced a seductive track down her backbone, sending delicious shivers of need feathering across her skin. 'Stay,' he urged sexily as his hand traced feather-light circles on her thigh.

It was impossible to refuse him. She gladly rolled back into the dark embrace of his welcoming arms. She had never felt happier, more fully alive, more certain that this was where she was meant to be. In this house, in this room, in this man's bed.

And she was still there when the phone on the bedside table rang shortly after dawn.

Byrne answered it on the second ring.

With his eyes narrowed against the emerging light, he relaxed back against the pillow and idly coiled a tendril of Fiona's hair around two fingers. 'Coolaroo.'

There was a beat, a short, suspended moment of normality, before Fiona sensed the sudden tension in him, felt her hair brush her bare skin as it dropped from his fingers.

Something was wrong. She felt a shaft of fear, almost a premonition.

'All right,' she heard Byrne say. 'I'll just get her.'

Oh, God. Whatever had happened involved her. At this hour, it could only be bad.

She shot upright, her heart leaping as she frantically searched for a clue in Byrne's darkened face.

Covering the receiver, he mouthed, 'It's for you.'

Her mind raced, trying to imagine what could possibly have happened.

'Who?' she whispered.

But Byrne simply handed her the receiver.

Her heart began a fretful hammering. 'Hello? Fiona speaking.'

'Fiona?' It was Samantha, her PA. 'I'm afraid I have bad news. Rex has had a stroke. It happened last night.'

'A stroke? Oh, heavens, the poor man. Where is he? Is it bad?'

'He's at the Royal North Shore hospital. I don't really know details yet. His wife was terribly upset when she rang. I don't think he's regained consciousness yet.'

'Oh, God, Sam. That's awful.'

'I'm sorry to ring so early, but I knew you'd want to make arrangements.'

'A-arrangements?'

'To fly back here as soon as you can.'

'Oh, yes. Of course.' Her gaze flew to Byrne, who was sitting poised on the edge of the bed, his body tense as if he was preparing to spring into action, his face serious, almost harsh.

'I think the Lear jet should be available,' Sam said.

The Lear jet could be here in a couple of hours. So soon.

Fiona pressed a hand to her mouth, sick at the thought of rushing away. From Byrne.

'Fiona?'

'Yes,' she said quickly. 'The Lear jet would be best. There's no airstrip here on Coolaroo, but it can land at the little airport at Gundawarra. I've used it before.'

'I'll ring back as soon as I have all the details.'

'Thanks, Sam.'

As Fiona handed the receiver back to Byrne she wanted to cry.

'It's Rex,' she said. 'He's had a stroke. I'm not sure, but it sounds like it might be bad.'

He nodded grimly.

'I'll have to go to Sydney.'

'Of course.'

He said this in such a matter-of-fact way that she felt her face scrunch up. Tears threatened. Byrne showed no sign that he cared at all that she was leaving him.

'I'm afraid I have no idea how long I'll be needed.'

Byrne frowned at her. 'How can you say that? You're not a casual employee. You're a partner in the company. You'll have to take over the reins.'

'Yes, but I thought—'

Byrne had left the bed and was dragging on jeans.

Heart sinking, Fiona tried again. 'I—I mean I'm going to miss you,' she said, but it felt so inadequate.

Byrne's jaw was as set as concrete. 'I just hope your partner pulls through,' he said. 'Don't give me a second thought.'

'How can you expect me not to think of you? Of course I'll give you a second thought. And probably a third and a fourth. Maybe a billion thoughts. What else would you expect?'

Her mouth pulled out of shape and she took a deep breath, swallowed to ease the painful ache in her throat, and wished she didn't feel quite so vulnerable, sitting naked in Byrne's bed while he stood there, clothed and scowling. 'Surely you don't think I can just walk away and forget you? Is that what you want?'

For a fleeting, unguarded moment, she saw a battle in his eyes. Regret and despair versus longing. But the impression came and went so quickly, she was left wondering if she'd imagined it.

Byrne's fist smashed into the palm of his other hand, then he shrugged almost insolently and refused to meet her gaze. 'You were always going back to the city. I knew that. It was just a matter of when. And, well, now it's happened. A bit sooner than we might have liked, and under regrettable circumstances, but perhaps, in the long run, it's for the best.'

'How can it be for the best?'

He shook his head at her, as if the answer was obvious.

Unable to bear the sudden lack of warmth in his gaze, she looked down and pulled the sheet high to cover her.

'I'll go and put the kettle on,' he said.

'Damn the kettle,' Fiona cried. 'I want to talk about us.'

'Ssh. You don't want to wake Scamp.'

Last night she'd been so happy, so sure that Byrne felt something for her. She'd dreamed of marrying him, had been willing to give up everything for him.

Now she wondered how she'd ever been so confident.

She had no doubts about her own feelings. She loved this man and she wanted to tell him that. Now. But the formidable chill in his face killed the words as they formed on her lips.

'Make the tea if you must.' She knew she sounded churlish, but she couldn't help it. 'I'll take a shower.'

* * *

The next few hours were horrendous. Byrne was solicitous, but in such a businesslike and efficient way that Fiona wanted to scream. Riley's response was more gratifying.

'I don't want you to leave,' she cried, and clung to Fiona, her eyes brimming.

In the end, Byrne was forced to reprimand his daughter, which made everyone feel terrible, and Riley left for school in Ted's ute with tears running down her cheeks.

Then it was Fiona's turn to leave for the airport with Byrne, and she had never felt more miserable than when she hugged Ellen.

'I'm real sorry to see you go.' Ellen sniffed, dragged a handkerchief from her apron pocket and dabbed it to her eyes.

Byrne tapped at the face of his wristwatch. 'Time to head off.' He spoke tersely and he opened the passenger door for Fiona and waited, without smiling, till she was seated.

As they headed down the dirt track leading away from the homestead, he kept silent, sat straight, both hands on the wheel and eyes fixed ahead, his face grim—with the kind of remote, distanced demeanour Fiona associated with the time before he'd rescued her from the fire.

But she couldn't bear to see him retreat from her again. Not after last night. She wouldn't accept it. Not without a fight.

'Why are you being like this?' she demanded, lifting her voice above the noise of their vehicle as it rattled over the unsealed bumpy track.

His eyes narrowed, but he didn't look at her. 'What do you mean?'

'Oh, Byrne, don't play games. You know exactly what I mean. You're keeping your distance, as if I'm just any old visitor you have to take to the airport, as if last night never happened.'

A dark colour tinged his cheekbones and the muscles in his throat worked. 'Last night should not have happened. I should have had more sense. And you've got to be sensible, now, Fiona. You've got to go back to Hartley & McLaren and forget about me.'

Appalled, she felt her mouth gape open. 'How can I forget about you? It's not possible.'

'Sure it is. Once you're back in the thick of things, you won't have time to think about us.'

He seemed so certain. Her throat hurt so badly, she thought she might gag. 'Is that what you want?'

'Yes.'

'Even if, say, in six months' time I could wind down my commitments?'

His brow furrowed into a shocked frown. 'How can you even think of winding down while Rex Hartley's so ill?'

Fiona blanched. Did he have to make her feel such a heel? It wasn't as if she didn't care about Rex, or the company. She did care, very much. But she cared about Byrne, too, loved him enough to give up everything else in her life.

It hurt to realise that his feelings for her were little more than simple lust. The thought of leaving him almost destroyed her.

A burning river of heat seared her chest and she

winced, took a deep breath, and tried to ease the pain. She'd almost forgotten about her heartburn over the past few days, but now it was back, nastier than ever.

They reached the main road, and Byrne turned left and the four-wheel-drive began to speed along the smooth bitumen towards Gundawarra. She thought of the first time she'd driven out along this road, when these stringy bark gum trees had seemed as unfamiliar as a moonscape.

If only she could turn back the clock to the night of the masked ball and have her time with Byrne all over again. If only she could handle things differently. Get it right.

As things stood, Byrne was probably relieved to be free of her, he probably felt she'd messed up his life. After all, she'd revealed devastating news about his relationship with his daughter, had interfered in his household, and dragged him away from his own property to help out at White Cliffs.

From his point of view, one fantastic night in bed couldn't possibly make up for the massive fall-out.

He didn't speak as the four-wheel-drive hurried to Gundawarra, and Fiona was too distraught to attempt idle chatter. She sat with her arms folded and turned her head to stare out the window. This country was so familiar to her now. She knew each dip in the road, each rattling wooden bridge across every creek, each rise to crest a rocky ridge.

She thought about her flat in Sydney, twenty floors up in a skyscraper, with cream fitted carpets, smooth white and mocha walls, a stainless steel kitchen, white marble bathroom, views of other skyscrapers and a miniscule glimpse of glittering Sydney harbour. She pictured herself there, sitting alone, eating take-away noodles with chopsticks from a cardboard carton, sipping a latte that she'd bought in a cardboard cup from the café on the ground floor while she sat working late into the night at her laptop.

If the truth were told, she hardly ever cooked the recipes she'd boasted about to Byrne. In Sydney her recipes were carefully filed on her computer, and her state-of-the-art stove with its wok burner and fan oven were as sparkling and spotless as the day she'd moved in. She never had time for cooking.

She thought about poor Rex. The dear man had to pull through. He'd worked hard all his life, and he deserved many happy years of retirement. She tried to think about all the work that lay ahead of her, the briefings, meetings, deadlines, but her mind kept shying away from all that. She didn't want to have to think about it. Not yet.

A faded, weatherboard house with a clothesline full of washing flashed past and she realised they were almost at Gundawarra. The airport was on the outskirts of town, and she felt a moment's panic.

Any minute now they would arrive, Byrne would despatch her with businesslike efficiency into the care of Hans the pilot, and there would be no chance for any kind of private farewell. Soon she would be gone from here.

She turned to Byrne, couldn't remain silent any longer. 'It's hard to believe I won't be coming back here.'

'You'll come back some time. You'll probably want to stay in touch with Riley.'

'Well, yes. That would be nice,' she said, but with such sad iciness that he flicked a cautious glance her way.

'I mean it,' he said. 'It would mean a lot to her if you could keep in touch.'

'I realise that, Byrne. It would mean a lot to me, too.' She blinked, ground her teeth together and willed herself not to cry. 'When's her birthday?'

For a moment he hesitated, and she forced a small, heartless laugh. 'I forgot; men never know their children's birthdays.'

'It's April the fifteenth.'

'Right,' she said, chastened. 'I'll remember that.'

And then, too soon, she saw the flat-topped building that housed the airport offices, the hangars nearby, the tarmac, the windsocks, and, at the end of the runway, the H&M Lear jet, ready and waiting.

Byrne turned the Land Cruiser in beneath a painted sign bidding them farewell from Gundawarra, and he parked in one of the many empty bays. He turned off the ignition, pulled on the handbrake and Fiona, impulsively, laid her hand over his.

'Just a moment,' she said, conscious of the sudden tension in the big brown hand beneath hers. 'I—I can't leave without being honest about my emotions and about how I feel about you.'

His face tightened and his eyes turned flint-hard. 'Fiona, I don't think—'

'This will only take a moment, Byrne.' She felt a desperate, panicking surge of helplessness and squeezed his hand, imploring him to be still for just that moment.

Their eyes met briefly, and Fiona saw sadness and

consternation in his. In the confines of the cabin she felt suddenly hot and dizzy. Ill. But she couldn't back down now.

'I understand that you would like this to be the end of our relationship,' she said quietly, in spite of the dreadful pounding of her heart.

She waited a beat and, when he nodded ever so slightly, she rushed on.

'I accept your choice, Byrne, but I'm not going to say it's OK. I'm not going to play this your way and be rational and adult. I need to be irrational about this. And I need to tell you that I'm in love.'

A small, choking sound erupted in his throat.

'I'm sorry,' she said, unable to see him now because of the hot tears blinding her. 'I know you probably don't want to hear this, but I had to tell you. I can't leave here without telling you how I feel. I love you, Byrne. I love you and Riley, and I always will.'

And then, because her outburst was embarrassing for both of them, she pushed the car door open and stumbled out into the glaring sunshine.

As she swiped at her damp face, she heard Byrne's car door open and then the thump of it shutting. Gravel crunched beneath his boots as he went to the back of the vehicle and removed the small bag that contained her few belongings, most of which he had provided.

She held her breath as he came round to her side of the vehicle. He looked grave, his eyes stricken grey chips of slate.

Oh, heavens. Had she been selfish to get her feelings off her chest? She'd already dumped so much grief on this man, and now she was burdening him with unsolicited declarations of undying love.

'Miss McLaren.'

There was a shout behind her and Hans, the Lear jet's pilot, hurried up to them, extending his hand to Fiona. 'Good to see you again.'

'And you, Hans. How's Rex? What's the latest?'

'Last we heard, about thirty minutes ago, he'd regained consciousness, but he was undergoing tests.'

'Right. We'll have to hope for the best, then.' Fiona nodded towards the waiting plane. 'You made good time.'

'Yes. I had to. We're on a very tight schedule today.'

Hans acknowledged Byrne with a polite nod, and Fiona made hasty introductions. The two men shook hands.

'I'm sorry to rush this,' Hans said, turning his attention back to Fiona. 'But I've instructions to get you back to Sydney as quickly as possible. Samantha Hale is in the plane.'

'Sam? On this plane?' Fiona squinted across the tarmac.

'Yes. She wants to use the flight back to Sydney to brief you, so you can head straight into important meetings this afternoon.' Hans winked. 'Lucky you.'

'Oh, yeah. Lucky me.' Fiona smiled ruefully. 'No time for fond farewells, then.' She turned back to Byrne, held out her hand. 'Thanks for all your help, Byrne.'

He reached for her shoulders, stooped and kissed her cheek. 'It's best this way,' he murmured close to her ear.

She clung to him, kept her cheek against his, needed to feel one more time the masculine roughness of his jaw against her skin. It didn't seem real, didn't seem possible that they could part like this.

But when she released him he stepped away smartly, almost like a soldier who'd delivered a salute. Hans took her bag.

'Where's the rest of your luggage?' he asked, frowning.

'It's a long story,' Fiona told him. 'Come on, let's go, and I'll explain on the way.'

Six weeks later, five days before Christmas, very important-looking mail with Sydney postmarks arrived at Coolaroo. A square box-shaped, brown paper parcel addressed in flowing, stylish handwriting to Miss Riley Drummond, and a fat Manila typed envelope for Byrne.

To Riley's dismay, her parcel went under the Christmas tree, not to be opened until December 25th, but Byrne took the envelope through to his study. He'd guessed its contents even before he opened it, but just the same the impersonal solicitor's letter, advising him that he and his daughter were now joint owners of White Cliffs, felt like a body blow.

He shook out the envelope, hoping for a note from Fiona, but there was nothing.

Nothing.

In six weeks, not a word.

Her silence was what he'd asked for, of course, but it bothered him more than he could have believed.

Losing his wife three years ago had been horrendous. But death, he realised now, was clear cut. Unequivocal. There was nothing he could do to bring Tessa back.

This was different.

To know that Fiona was living, laughing, sleeping

and waking, to know that she was an e-mail, a phone call, a plane flight away in Sydney and to have no contact whatsoever, was torture beyond imagining.

And now this aloof and formal document from her solicitors.

Becoming the owner of White Cliffs should have been cause for celebration.

Byrne threw the documents aside and kicked at a chair, strode to the window. Stared out. And knew he'd been a fool for long enough.

CHAPTER ELEVEN

IT DIDN'T make sense.

There were no lights in the offices of Hartley & McLaren, no people behind the sleek teak desks. And when Byrne pushed at the huge plate-glass doors he discovered they were locked.

He checked again the company's name, painted in fancy gold lettering on the glass: *Hartley & McLaren, Marketing and Media Consultants.* This had to be the office where Fiona worked. But why was it closed? It wasn't a public holiday.

He'd been concerned when he couldn't get an answer on Fiona's mobile, had been anxious when no one answered at the address she'd listed on the sale documents for White Cliffs, and now he was really worried.

Trying to ignore a growing sense of panic, he hurried to the reception desk of the business next door, and had to wait impatiently until a girl with blonde and purple striped hair finished a phone conversation that sounded more social than business.

'How can I help you, sir?' She flashed him a frank up-and-down appraisal and a sparkling smile.

'I'm looking for Hartley & McLaren,' he said. 'Have they moved premises?'

Her eyes widened with surprise. 'Where have you been for the past month? Haven't you heard?'

'Heard what?' he snapped.

'There was a takeover. Southern Developments bought out H & M.'

Byrne swallowed a knot of something that felt like glass shards. 'What happened to the people who worked there? Where have they gone?'

The girl shrugged and reached for a nail file. 'Anyone's guess. It happened suddenly. I don't know. Sorry.'

He spent the night pacing his hotel room, cursing himself for being such a fool.

Over and over he kept seeing Fiona, standing proud and courageous at the Gundawarra airport.

I love you...and I always will.

She'd been so gutsy and emotionally honest. And how had he responded?

With fear.

He'd let her go because he'd been too afraid to sort through his confused emotions, had been too thick-headed to recognize the simple truth shining through all the complexities. Fiona loved him. And he loved her.

He did.

He loved her.

Fiona had known it. She was one smart, classy woman, and she'd taken the risk to speak out because she believed that he loved her.

Too late, he'd faced the joyous, frightening truth. He loved Fiona McLaren.

And he'd sent her packing.

How stupid was that? What kind of idiot made the same mistake twice?

Last time he'd paid a painful price for letting Tessa go and waiting too long to find her. This time he was facing even greater heartbreak.

This time it was very obvious that Fiona didn't want to be found. Unless…

As he reached for the telephone book, Byrne knew he had one last chance.

'Buonasera, signorina.'

'Buonasera, Luigi.' Fiona offered a slight dip of her head to acknowledge the waiter's more lavish bow, and then followed him through the hotel's restaurant to the table near the big arched window overlooking Lake Como.

'And how are you enjoying the most beautiful part of Italy?' Luigi enquired in careful English as he drew out her chair.

'I'm loving it, thank you. The weather's perfect, and I've walked and walked.'

'And shopped?' The waiter cast a practised eye over the elegant cream silk trouser suit she'd found in one of the little boutiques that hugged the cobbled, stepped streets.

'Yes, do you like this?'

Luigi smiled, and kissed two fingers curled in a circle. *'Magnifico.'* But then his lustrous, dark Italian eyes reproached her. 'But, in Bellagio, the most romantic town in all of Italy, you should not be alone, signorina.'

With a light laugh and a dismissive toss of her head, Fiona held out her hand for the menu. 'I'm more interested in tasting another of your divine meals than in romance.'

And what a bald-faced lie that was.

As Luigi handed her the menu and filled her water glass, she struggled to hold her smile in place. Once he'd departed, she let out a deep, heart-shuddering sigh.

Here she was in Italy, a country she'd always longed to visit, and she was supposed to be happy, having the time of her life. But she suspected she might never be happy again.

Leaving the menu unopened, she stared out through the window and made an effort to concentrate on being happy. She should be happy. It was so lovely here. Even at night the view was pretty. In the floodlit gardens below, the azaleas provided spectacular splashes of colour, and the lights scattered around the lake's edge looked like diamonds in a necklace, grouping into clusters where small towns climbed the lakeside slopes.

Every day since she'd arrived, the winter weather had been perfect, crystal-clear and crisp, each day more beautiful than the last. This morning, she'd eaten break-fast on a flower-adorned terrace with a view of the distant snow-capped Alps silhouetted against the pale morning sky. She'd watched small sailboats setting off across the lapis-blue lake and had admired the wooded hills sweeping upward from the shore, the picturesque scattering of villas with colourful roof tops of ochre, burnt sienna and yellow.

But she'd almost wept with loneliness.

She'd come here to forget Byrne, had chosen this perfect setting, this refined hotel run by the same Italian family for over a century, in the hope that the relaxing old-world, totally un-Australian atmosphere would help her to heal, to restore her sense of balance.

It wasn't working.

Tonight she couldn't even dredge up an appetite for the mouth-watering selections offered on the fabulous menu.

Listlessly, she took a sip of iced water, traced the menu's embossed leather cover with lethargic fingertips, thought about going back to her room without eating. But it would be foolish to try to sleep on an empty stomach. Sighing again, she flipped the menu open, cast a languid glance at the list.

And blinked.

Instead of the usual range of Italian courses— L'antipasto, Il primo, Il secondo, Il contorno, Il dolce— the page was almost blank, save for one dish listed square in the middle.

Spaghetti Bolognese.

Frowning, she turned the page.

Just two words sat in the middle of the next sheet of white paper.

Green jelly.

A frightening, thrilled kind of panic gripped her heart, and the water glass slipped from her fingers.

Surely not.

Surely Byrne couldn't have done this.

But who else? She'd never eaten spaghetti Bolognese and green jelly with anyone but him.

Trembling, she righted the glass and made hasty dabs at the puddle with her napkin, while she cast frantic glances around the diners, searching the scattered tables for a tall and rangy, tanned Australian.

When she couldn't find him, she jumped to her feet and scanned every square inch of the restaurant, not caring that she attracted attention.

But there was no sign of Byrne.

She glanced again at the menu, and then looked for Luigi, who was on the far side of the room with his back to her, busily delivering bowls of soup to another set of diners.

Her heart thumped wildly as she sat down again and turned back to the first page of the menu, searching for a clue. This had to be some kind of weird coincidence. Surely it was a local novelty dish for a religious festival, or something like that.

Leafing forward again, she discovered a third page in the menu that she hadn't noticed before.

And in the middle of it, a typed message: *This selection is served in Room 267 only.*

Good heavens.

Was she going mad? Her pulse leapt frenetically as she flipped through the pages once more, double-checking each item. Spaghetti Bolognese, green jelly, room 267.

A hailstorm of emotions besieged her, and she couldn't think clearly. But she kept coming back to Byrne.

Pressing one hand against the savage beating in her chest, she turned in her seat and tried again to catch Luigi's eye. After all, he'd handed her this menu, this particular menu, so he must know the story behind it.

But Luigi, usually the most attentive of waiters, was suddenly exceptionally busy. Every time Fiona tried to wave or beckon, he was detained by yet another small task.

It was too much. She couldn't possibly sit still. Snatching up her chic, new evening purse, she jumped to her feet, hurried through the restaurant and out into the marbled and mirrored foyer where she punched a button for the lift.

It arrived promptly, its doors separating with a discreet swish, and her knees shook so badly she almost stumbled. An elderly couple frowned at her as if she was drunk.

'Excuse me,' she murmured, and pressed the button for the second floor.

The ancient lift climbed with agonising slowness, and Fiona studied her reflection in the mirrored back wall, grateful that she'd taken trouble with her appearance. But her eyes looked glassy with shock, her cheeks far too bright.

And then, at last, too soon, the lift stopped on level two. The doors opened, and somehow her limbs found the ability to move. She stepped out into the carpeted hallway, saw room 267 almost immediately.

Oh, help. Who was waiting on the other side of that door?

Please... please...

Drawing a swift, deep breath for courage, she straightened her shoulders and crossed the hallway. Her heart pounded so loudly it almost drowned out her knock.

She closed her eyes, praying that it would be Byrne who opened the door. If it wasn't him, she might die of disappointment.

The door opened and a tall, dark figure stood there, framed in the doorway.

A young Italian. A complete stranger.

'Oh.' Fiona gasped.

His eyes widened with surprise.

'I'm sorry,' she mumbled miserably. 'I think I've made a mistake.'

The young man smiled and bowed. With a gesture of welcome, he pushed the door further open. *'Buonasera, signorina. Entri prego.'*

And then, as she took a tentative step forward, he slipped out into the corridor and she realised he was a part of the hotel's room-service staff.

And waiting, inside the room, stood another man.

Tall, dark, bronzed and absolutely gorgeous in a black dinner suit, white shirt and bow tie.

He smiled uncertainly. 'Hello, Fiona.'

Fiona couldn't move for fear she would break the spell and he would disappear.

'I thought it had to be you,' she managed shakily. 'H-how?' she stuttered. 'Why?'

For answer, Byrne stepped towards her, his arms open, and with a hiccuping little cry of joy she fell into his welcoming embrace and burst into tears.

'Darling girl,' Byrne murmured as he shouldered the door shut and held her close, stroked her hair, kissed her damp eyelids.

Fiona clung to him, hardly able to believe that this was really happening. Byrne, here. Byrne, really here. Now. It was like waking up in the middle of a dream. These strong arms around her were Byrne's. This rock-like shoulder, these gentle hands, that crisp, clean scent, these warm lips. All of it, him.

Laughing through her tears, she looked up. 'I can't quite believe this.' And suddenly, as if a gong had been struck, her mind filled with questions.

'Where's Riley?'

'Right here in room 103, watching movies with a sitter.'

She shot him a puzzled smile. 'Are you here on holiday? On some kind of business trip?'

He looked suddenly shy. 'I—I've been trying to work up a beautiful speech to explain, I've been frantically searching for you.'

'When I saw the menu, I—I was—I was terrified I was wrong. I—'

Byrne stopped her babbling with a finger on her lips. His eyes shimmered. 'I came here to tell you that I love you, Fiona.'

And then, before she could respond, he lowered his face to hers, and everything he wanted to say was expressed through the reverence of his kiss.

And as Fiona kissed him back she felt incredibly free, free in a way she'd never felt before. Free to love this man, to be herself, find herself.

Their kiss lasted a deliciously long time.

When they eventually broke apart, she glanced past Byrne's shoulder and saw a table just like the one she'd recently vacated, set by a lace-curtained window, with starched white linen, gleaming silver, a little vase of purple Alpine irises, and to one side an ice bucket with champagne.

She grinned so broadly, she thought her face might split. 'How romantic.'

She laughed, shook her head in amazement. And then remembered another niggling question. 'Byrne, how on earth did you find me?'

'With great difficulty.'

Grabbing his hands, she gave them an impatient little shake. 'Tell me. What happened?'

'When I couldn't get an answer on your phone, I went to Sydney and rocked up to Hartley & McLaren, only to discover that your offices were empty. The girl in the place next door told me you'd been taken over.'

'That wasn't quite right.'

'So I discovered.' Drawing her close again, Byrne kissed her forehead, caressed the side of her head with his jaw. 'I spent a day and a night stalking your apartment.'

'Oh dear,' she said, not quite managing to hide her delight.

'Eventually, in desperation, I rang Rex Hartley.'

'And what did he say?'

'You want his exact words?'

'Yes.'

'"It's about bloody time, son",' he said, mimicking Rex's gravelly voice almost exactly. '"I was about to ring you".'

Fiona pulled away to get a better look at Byrne's face. 'Did Rex deliver a lecture?'

Byrne smiled down at her. 'At great length. He told me that the two of you had sold up your business so he could retire and you could travel the world, and that I was seven versions of a fool for letting you go. He spent quite a long time bawling me out, and telling me that I didn't deserve you, and then he gave me minute details of exactly how to find you and said if I let you down again I'd have him to answer to.'

Byrne tipped Fiona's chin upwards and smiled straight into her eyes, making her melt from head to toe.

'You've travelled all this way,' she said.

'I would have crossed the Sahara Desert in bare feet if I had to. I love you, Fiona. Please believe it. I should have told you when you were at Coolaroo, but I didn't want you to give up your career. It wasn't till later that I realised that I could have you if I sold Coolaroo.'

She pulled away, appalled. 'You haven't. You can't do that. Please tell me you haven't sold your home.'

'No, not yet. But I would, if it was the only way I could be with you.'

'Oh, my.' Fiona felt teary again. She laid her hand tenderly against his cheek. 'If only you'd asked me, Byrne. I would have told you I was hoping for a career change.'

'You were?' His brow furrowed, and his eyes narrowed warily. 'What's your new plan?'

She smiled and nestled closer, linked her hands around his neck. In a husky whisper, she ordered, 'Kiss me, Byrne, and I'll show you.'

His face broke into a smile and, cradling her face with both hands, he obeyed her.

'Any more orders?' he murmured, trailing sweet kisses down her neck.

But Fiona was quite certain there had been enough words. Later, there would be plenty of time over dinner to tell him about the brilliant eco-tourism ideas she'd had for White Cliffs.

For now, she had more urgent plans for the man she loved.

Grasping his jacket by the lapels, she drew Byrne deeper into the room, and she kissed him in a way that shouted her joy, her love and her eagerness to be in bed with him already.

Byrne got the message. Loud and clear.